REPTILES VS AMPHIBIANS

Published by Mindstir Media, LLC

1931 Woodbury Ave. #182 | Portsmouth, New Hampshire 03801 | USA

1.800.767.0531 | www.mindstirmedia.com

Printed in the United States of America

ISBN-13: 978-0-9970334-6-5

Library of Congress Control Number: 2015919614

REPTILES VS AMPHIBIANS

CHELCIE C. OPARANOZIE

MINDSTIR MEDIA

DEDICATED TO

My dad George, my mom Obioma, my little sister Daisy, my little brother Justice, and my grandparents Felicitas, Augustine, Eugene and Imelda.

And to all the people that will read this book. You are really helping me out as a starting author. I was 11-years-old when I wrote this book and I was very nervous. Words can barely describe it, but words could never express my happiness. I can't wait to not only finish the series, but to make many more books in the future.

INTRODUCTION

In the year 2040, there were a few American citizens who were half-reptiles/half-humans or half-amphibians/half-humans located in different parts of the country. The Americans were scared and concerned about these different-looking creatures. People's concerns and fears led the United States Government to round up all the unusual creatures and ship them to a country distant from the rest of North America.

A toxic waste factory located in Middle America was destroyed in a massive earthquake. All of the containers in the factory, along with radioactive chemicals, leaked into the river and the water supply across America became extremely polluted. People started dying from drinking the polluted water. The chemicals started killing animals. Eventually, the animal corpses started settling on undersea explosives, People were initially unaware of the undersea explosives and how they got there. What the Americans didn't know, and were unprepared for, was the undersea explosives blowing up, causing floods across the nation and drowning the whole country. The people panicked and some fled the United States.

The United States Government was not only losing citizens, but losing money and the entire economy was collapsing. The government was losing control of its citizens and the economy. The remaining Americans, who did not flee to other countries outside the United States, got thousands of boats, ships, planes, helicopters, and submarines and began looking for a new land in exploration manner.

Ultimately, the Americans discovered a lost country known

as Phenise with around ten states. The only problem was, it had already been taken over by two tribes. One tribe was known as the Reptiles and the other tribe, Amphibians. The tribes originated from the United States when the United States Government rounded up the weird and odd-looking creatures and shipped them to the deserted island. Years later, Americans discovered Phenise, which happened to be the same place the creatures were shipped.

The Reptiles were brave warriors and stealth agents who taught their descendants to be alert, aware, and athletic. Each Reptile goes to extreme training camps far away from their homes around the age of four to eight and stays there for at least 10 to 12 years. This is where they learn combat, detective skills, and how to strategize. Then they are assigned into teams of four. The Reptiles are known for being half-reptile, half-human hybrids.

The average Reptile organizations are made up of two groups of four in each state. When a member from either group dies, they are replaced with a new recruit from the training camp.

The second tribe is the Amphibians. Not much is known about them. The rule that they live by is to be adverse, aggressive, and armed with weapons. They are known to retreat from battle easily. This is so they can focus on hiding their identities. If they are in battle for too long, the enemy might learn their faces and track them down. The Amphibians are half-amphibian, half-human.

The Amphibian tribe is similar to an organization with a leader and thousands of ninjas as army members.

The way that the humanoid-animal hybrids – the Reptiles and Amphibians - were mutated remains a mystery, but there have been rumors of government experiments gone wrong, natural creations, and even the results of bestiality. The most common rumor is that a few humans worked at a chemical manufacturing factory, but accidently fell into the containers. Another rumor is that some humans deliberately fell because they thought that being a mutant would get them more attention. Either way, all of the mutants were sent to Phenise and banned to come back to America ever again, because they were scaring Americans.

Phenise was taken off all of the maps, after the original shipment of the mutants, and completely erased from all human knowledge until the humans found them again.

The mutants were surprisingly welcoming to the American people, and let them stay to trade and to live. Unfortunately, the Americans took over, and the place became overpopulated with humans. Now, Phenise is Ninety Percent human. The humans are referred to as "The Naturals" by the mutants

Forestry Evergreen High North is a very busy and violent school. It has a capacity of 1,096 students and 90 staff members (teachers, janitor, secretaries, the principal, and vice principal).

There are four dorm areas, two for the boys, and two for the girls. Then, there are two staff quarters. There are also nearby apartments off campus where some students and staff can live. At this school, students can study zoology, ecology, and geography. Ninety-five percent of the students are humans and five percent are Reptilians and Amphibians combined.

Alas, it is a place of hostility, betrayal, and war on the inside. No one knows why it's like this. On the outside, the school is so peaceful. It's on a separate island in Phenise called Creatoigin (cree-toh-ijin) Island, which has twenty towns. Forestry Evergreen is located in the capital, Snida.

CHAPTER 1

THE REPTILES' MISSION

There is a group of four friends that attends the school and protects the innocent people that go there. These teenagers are one of the two groups in the Reptilian Tribe.

The first member and leader is a boy named Thorn Woodland. He is 17 years old. Thorn is half-reptile like all his friends. He is half-snake, half-human. Thorn is the oldest and the most strategic member. However, his wisdom towards everything makes his friends a bit envious of him, so they refuse to listen to him at times.

Then there is Camilia Veildson, the second member and the most academically intelligent member. She is 15 years old. She is half-chameleon with chameleon eyes and the ability to change colors. But, she is a bit obsessed with her academics, which causes her to be quite distractible and absentminded.

The third member of the group is Pyro Nilowski, half-crocodile, half-human. He was named Pyro because he's actually a rare species of crocodile-humans called the Ignitodiles who create fire. He is the only known Ignitodile in his family. He is 14 years old and has fire spawning abilities. He is a determined, adventurous, free-spirited member of the group. His carefree attitude usually makes him the most gullible.

Finally, the fourth member is Geckeliette Frecklin. Everyone calls her Geck. Geck is 14 years old, half-gecko, half-human, she is brave and nimble, making her quick on her feet. At times, her curiosity tends to hold her back, and distracts Geck from important missions.

It was an early September morning; Camilia woke up and sprang from her bed in the dorm. She got all dressed up and woke her roommate, Geck.

Camilia said, "Get up, Geck! We have to get to the training room early for strategy planning before class starts."

Geck sat up and started groaning, "It's not fair! Why do we have to wake up so early?" She collapsed into her bed.

Camilia pulled her onto the floor and replied, "C'mon! We're going to be late! We still haven't finished the case of the missing teachers!"

Geck got ready and they both headed down to the hideout where they met up with Thorn and Pyro. Thorn said, "No time for strategy planning, now. We just got a glimpse of the security camera. Those Amphibians are back. We have to go immediately."

Geck complained, "Can we at least get something to eat, first? We never eat breakfast, always skip lunch, and by the time we get back for dinner, we already have to go to sleep!"

Then Pyro replied, "Deal with it! You think *you* have it bad? Me and Thorn have to wait two hours just for you guys to get down here every day! And also..."

Thorn interrupted him, "Eating is not an option. Freedom and heroics come before food and hunger; because without freedom and heroics, there would be no eating."

The others rolled their eyes. It made them upset how Thorn always came up with these wise sayings off the top of his head, especially because they were true.

As they were in the floating RV, they were talking about the case of the missing teachers. Floating RV's were very common in that period of time.

"I don't get it!" cried Geck. "Why have we been doing this missing teacher thing for months and we never even get to take any action?"

"This is a very complicated case, Geck. We don't know where they can be hiding, so we need to stay alert as to who could be taking them. Besides, we already have our suspicions about the Amphibians. They've been stealing from villages everywhere!" Camilia explained.

The four of them have been working on the case of the missing teachers for months. This started back in the summer, before school had started. All of the staff were wondering where Mr. Smith, the janitor, had gone. The teachers suspected that he had moved, but eventually, Mrs. Thomson, then Mr. Davis, and Ms. Jackson were nowhere to be seen. Soon, Principal Louis had the police start a search for the missing staff, but not even the cops could find them after two months. They are still searching, but still no use. One day, Thorn overheard some of the teachers talking when he went to reregister into the school.

"What are the Amphibians even stealing from the villagers?" Pyro asked.

"Well, they've stolen money, clothes, food, lives; the usual. But, we shouldn't worry too much about it. The town will be okay," Camilia replied.

Thorn, who was driving said, "There's a wise saying that Sensei Sudoku told me before we left to go to Creatoigin Island."

"And what's that?" Pyro asked.

"If the burglar is smiling, he has probably stolen your wallet," Thorn said.

Everyone in the van remained silent as they continued their search for the Amphibians. Then Pyro said once again. "And… what's *that?*"

"Not everything is as it seems," Thorn replied. "Camilia, which village is it this time?"

Camilia looked at her radar, which she carries with her all the time, and said, "It looks like the Panic O' Meter is pointing towards

Dirtstown Village."

"Dirtstown is a small village. We'll have to speed up."

Dirtstown Village is a small town in Creatoigin Island. Its population is around 1,050 people. The people of Dirtstown are known for being robbed the most by the Amphibians.

Pyro looked at Camilia, the Panic O' Meter App on her phone, and back at Camilia and said, "You have a Panic O' meter app?"

"I like to be aware of my surroundings?" Camilia said sharply. "Nerd," Pyro murmured under his breath. "Yeah, well, I'm not the one obsessed with zombie movies and games, comics, and toys!"

Pyro hid his zombie plush doll behind his back and said, "Correction, cinema flicks, playable recreation, graphic novels, and deluxe action figures!"

Once the team got to Dirtstown, they saw madness. Windows were shattered and roofs were sliding off of the buildings. No citizens were visible, because they were all hiding.

One of the shortest ninja's from the Amphibians, named Steve, walked up to Thorn and said, "So kid, I see you got your little 'squad' here. That's adorable, but maybe you all should scamper your Reptilian butts back to your Swamp!"

"Camilia, round up the citizens. Geck, defend the citizens," Thorn said and looked up at the bell tower, "I'll take care of the bell."

Before they each stormed off, Pyro grabbed Thorn's shoulder. "Don't I get to do anything? Maybe I can help with…"

Thorn backed away slowly. "Maybe you can…distract this guy!" Thorn said pointing at Steve. Thorn didn't really care about Steve, but he needed Pyro to stay out of trouble and not mess up the mission. Pyro nodded obediently and replied, "Oh, okay. I'll just stay here." Thorn nodded back and sprinted off.

Camilia tried running around and getting the citizens to cooperate, but no such luck. Then, she saw the mayor hiding under the bridge. She walked up to him and said, "Hey, Mr. Mayor!" The Mayor looked up and blushed profusely.

Camilia explained to the mayor that he should round up all the citizens to the bell tower for her.

Meanwhile, Geck was trying to fight off all the ninjas that were running towards her with daggers. "Please! Stop! Halt! Cease! Don't move!" Geck shouted at them. They kept coming.

They began to tackle her aggressively, trying to choke her. "You forced me to do this!" Geck removed her hairpin and shoved it down one ninja's throat. Then she drop kicked him into the air, and his chest blasted open, leaving the premises covered in blood. The ninjas bowed down and surrendered. "Good. Now go stand by the bell tower!" she instructed.

Geck put her extra hairpin in her purse and said to herself, "Wow, I guess I keep mixing up my hairpins. No wonder my friends don't like me doing their hair at slumber parties!"

Pyro and Steve were just sitting and staring at each other in disgust. Finally, Steve spoke, "What's your problem?"

Pyro shrugged. "You wouldn't get it."

"Talk to me, kiddo!" Steve insisted. They both sat on the ground. "I wish Thorn would let me help for once. It might have something to do with..." Steve interrupted, "You're an Ignitodile? I can tell. You have the eyes."

Pyro smiled excitedly. "What would you do?" Steve winked at him. "Okay, this isn't some be-yourself-and-follow your dreams crap. This is real life, man. I remember when I was like you. Young, insecure, and confused. Life wasn't easy. My wife left with my kid, money, and car. Once the tax collector started 'crying', I got kicked onto the streets in a blink. Eventually, I found a bag of crack on the road next to a corpse. So I..."

Pyro cringed, "Could you tell me what you did to feel secure again, without all of the gruesome details?"

"No, listen! I sold the bag to an ex-cop, he told his friends, and I was making dough every second! My point is, find something you're good at and embrace it! I found out I was a good salesman. One day, I decided to quit," Steve admitted solemnly.

"What happened?" Pyro asked, with eyes widening. "I ended up working for the Amphibians. That Thorn guy can go to heck. This is about you!" Steve said.

Pyro nodded. "You are right, Steve. Thanks for the advice … and possible nightmares." Steve chuckled and began to sharpen his ax.

All fifty ninjas were in one large group surrounding the townsfolk around the bell tower.

Thorn, who was next to the gigantic bell, tried pushing it down, but no use. He looked down and saw that the citizens were only a few steps away from the Amphibian group.

Thorn looked up and noticed a rope holding the bell to prevent it from falling.

Thorn cut the rope, and kicked the golden bell as hard as he could, then he jumped off, and landed swiftly onto the concrete in the bell tower. The bell rang louder than ever, and it fell on the concrete, and rolled out of the bell tower window.

It fell right on top of all of the ninjas, crushing them. The citizens cheered and went back to their farms to grow new crops to replace the stolen.

The Reptiles got back in the van and drove off, but not without taking Steve along with them.

In the team van, Thorn drove, Camilia read directions, and Geck and Pyro were interrogating Steve.

"Where is your master? Why are you stealing from the villagers? Where is your hideout?" Geck wouldn't stop hurling questions at poor Steve.

"Steve, we just want to know where your master is so that we can make peace with him. That way, he'll stop attacking the villagers," Pyro said calmly.

Steve just rolled his eyes and snorted, "You can't make me sing!" Thorn stopped the van. "Where does your leader live?" he asked. Steve bowed his head and let out a fake cry, "Please don't let my boss fire me! I thought you were the good guys!" Pyro was the only one who had pity on him and replied, "Well, we are the good guys. Maybe we could let him go?" Everyone stared at him for a full minute, until Geck said, "Shut up, Pyro. Of course we're the good guys. That's why we'll do anything it takes to secure justice for all, right?"

"I guess," Pyro murmured shyly.

Steve was happy that Pyro was standing up for him, and Steve gave them the directions to a nearby temple where the master was hiding.

The Reptiles and Steve drove off to the Temple.

CHAPTER 2

THE AMPHIBIANS' MISSION

The Reptiles reached the destination, the Temple, and released Steve and he walked back home. When they went up to the door, the temple was locked.

The Amphibians, who became aware that the Reptiles were attempting to enter the Temple, began plotting their attack against the Reptiles. Inside the Temple, the four main managers were plotting their attack strategy.

The first main member was the leader, Scat. He was a man with frog-eyes and green skin.

The second was his wife, Scurry. She was also a frog-human hybrid. She was in charge of the financial system.

The third was Gallant, the leader of the ninja armies.

The fourth was Scat and Scurry's daughter, Iguan. She was different. She was actually an Iguana-human hybrid.

"Those Reptiles always get away with stopping our pathetic army!" Scat cried.

Gallant stood and saluted Scat boldly, "Do not worry, leader. I shall defend you!"

"Sit down!" Scat roared at Gallant.

"Sweetheart, calm down! Getting a new army would simply cost too much money!" Scurry pleaded.

Iguan, Scat's daughter, got up from her seat and said, "Excuse me, I have a suggestion." She pointed to the chalkboard in the front of the room. In red chalk, it said, "Reptiles" but it had a red X on it. "If we send half of the armies to destroy villages, while the other half kidnaps teachers, then the Reptiles will be too overwhelmed with work, they'll just quit!"

"That's genius!" Scat said. "Hand me my cape, dear!"

Scurry gave him his cape and Scat walked out the front door of the temple to see the four Reptiles that he's been waiting for. He scowled at the Reptiles generally, and then Thorn particularly. He had plans for him. "Well, I guess it wouldn't hurt to beat four more brats up. Gallant call the ninjas! These Reptiles will be too easy to destroy!" Scat insisted.

"Untrue! If the chipmunk sprouts wings, then it is most likely not a chipmunk! You should never inform your opponents," Thorn replied angrily as he threw his throwing stars at Scat, knocking off his helmet.

"You are braver than I gave you credit for, young warrior," Scat said. "But you have many more challenges that await you, Thorn. That's how you fell for our trap! While you and your minions were saving that petty village and the villagers, half of my army has gone to terrorize Forestry Evergreen High School!"

"How do you know my name? Who are you? Why are you... wait! You're the one kidnapping the teachers?" Thorn questioned Scat. Then calmed down and spoke to his members, "Team, split up. Camilia and Pyro, you two go back to the school and take down those ninjas. Geck and I will make sure this guy knows what we want."

"They call me...Scat." He came out of his shadow, a man with green scales and frog eyes.

"An Amphibian, what do we do, Thorn?" cried Geck. "Follow my lead," Thorn whispered. "Alright! We surrender!" He shouted out, dropping his katana sword. Geck did the same, confused about what the plan was.

Two Amphibian henchman lifted Geck and Thorn by the arms and carried them to the inside of the temple door, where Scat sat on his throne.

"Kneel!" He told them. They did as he asked. "Good. You are obedient. See here, you will never ask to make peace with me. You will never come near my temple again. You will never get in the way of my armies raiding the villages. Alright?"

"Okay," Thorn and Geck agreed in sync and left. Once they were taken outside of the temple, Geck asked, "Why did we do that?" Thorn looked behind his shoulder and said, "Now, we have his hopes up. He won't suspect us returning. Let's go meet up with Camilia and Pyro."

Meanwhile, Camilia and Pyro were at the school.

"Do you think zombies took the teachers?" Pyro asked Camilia.

"Zombies aren't real, Pyro. I wish Thorn were here. He'd know where to look for ninjas in this school," Camilia sighed.

"Yeah, you do wish Thorn was here. But life sucks, because you got stuck with me," Pyro mocked her, elbowing her in her side.

"For one thing he's way less annoying than *you!*" Camilia mumbled, ready to grab Pyro and throw him out the window.

Then they heard footsteps from around the corner and got their weapons out. "Where is everyone?" Pyro asked Camilia. "Today's that huge all-student field trip to some amusement park," Camilia responded. Pyro nodded and replied, "And the staff?"

Camilia shrugged and said, "Either on vacation or at the amusement park. But, that's not important. Those footstep noises might've been an Amphibian!"

To no one's surprise, it was. The leader of the ninjas, Gallant, confronted them and said, "Hey, Reptiles, where is everyone?"

Camilia flipped her ponytail aside and scoffed, "Like we'd tell you? We're not doing your dirty work, Amphibian!" Gallant scratched his toad-like green arm and snorted, "Be that way! That's just a fancy way of saying you don't know, Reptile!"

Pyro saw a potential fight and tried to end it, "Come on, Camilia, let's just go. He obviously couldn't find any other Amphibians who care." Gallant walked out the door and into his truck. He thought of a better plan as he drove off, back to the temple.

Camilia and Pyro headed back to Scat's temple, where they met up with Thorn and Geck. "We should go check up with the south side. They might need our help," said Thorn.

There is another team on the south campus of Forestry Evergreen High. They keep that place safe from the Amphibians. The leader is a boy named Repto Plummedly. He is 18 and half-basilisk lizard, half-human.

His sister is 17-year-old Lizzy Plummedly who is half-human, half-basilisk lizard as well. Lizzy is a bit mentally challenged, but she is a good fighter. After suffering a head trauma while in a battle, Lizzy became very naïve.

Next there is 15-year-old Mishell Snapper, who dons a shell on her back. Mishell is known to be the peacemaker and humanist of her friends. She was rescued by the northern team when her village was under attack. She is half-turtle, half-human, but is actually pretty fast on her feet.

The last and youngest member is 8-year-old Scales Nilowski, Pyro's little brother who is just like him. They share the same facial qualities and personality. Scales, due to his abnormally high I.Q., is in the 9th grade.

Thorn, Camilia, Pyro, and Geck went to the southern hideout.

Thorn knocked on the door. No one answered, so he just kicked it down. The four of them saw Repto curled up in a fetal position, tears in his eyes, breathing heavily, mumbling, "Just don't think about it. Just don't think about it!" repeatedly.

Geck immediately screeched, "Repto, are you okay?"

Repto slowly got up and stuttered, "Y...you guys should've come earlier...before it happened."

"What happened?" asked Camilia.

"Just follow me," Repto nervously replied. They followed him to the basement.

In the basement, they saw Lizzy, who was nailing wooden planks to the window. She had a traumatized look on her face as if she had seen a friend die in a train wreck. "Those stupid Amphibians took everything!" she growled as she took her last piece of wood and hammered both ends into the broken window.

She pointed at the floor where there was broken glass, spilled food, and a sharp knife with red stains on it.

Geck had a strange feeling about the disastrous mess of glass and red liquid. "Wait, I understand the broken glass, but how did the blood get there? And when did this all happen? It looks like the glass spells out something!" Geck pointed out. Thorn squinted at the mess on the ground and said, "It's a different language. Camilia, take notes."

Camilia took out her notepad and followed his command, writing down what they witnessed.

Scales walked into the room. He immediately exclaimed, "You guys missed it! We totally got robbed! A bunch of ninjas with frog-like heads must've snuck in somehow, because we woke up and found them here, taking our furniture and food! We tried to fight them off, but they escaped with most of our stuff."

"Okay, what happened next?" asked Thorn.

"Repto got one of the Amphibian ninjas to admit they worked for a frog-man named Scat who lives in a temple! We were just about to go after them, but we wanted to secure everything and make sure they don't come back!" cried Mishell, who was handing planks of wood to Lizzy.

Thorn shook his head in disgust and said, "Scat! So *he* did this. Don't worry guys. Keep guarding this school. We'll get your stuff back."

So the four friends left the South team hideout base and went back to the temple to try and retrieve their friends' belongings.

CHAPTER 3

THE BREAK IN

Once they arrived at the temple, an army of ninja toad-men were guarding the temple. "Okay, we'll have to try the back door. Geck, you distract the guards," Thorn said.

"I wanted to sneak around back!" Geck whined, "I want to see what's back there!"

"Look on the bright side, Geck. You're the fastest, so you're the least likely to get caught or killed!" Camilia tried to comfort her friend. Geck pouted stubbornly and nodded.

Geck donned her hood and walked up to the two frog-men. "Hey, I saw a Reptile climb up that window up there!" she insisted, pretending to be another Amphibian. She pointed to a window on the highest floor. "You better go get a ladder."

The gullible security guards obeyed her and got in their car. They drove off to get a ladder.

Meanwhile, the back door to the temple was locked. "How are we going to open a steel door?" Pyro asked. Camilia grinned widely and replied, "Not to worry. I brought my D.D.D. with me."

Thorn stared at the door and responded, "Camilia, I don't even want to know what that is." Camilia explained anyway, "It stands for door detaching device. I just put this magnet on the door and the door falls out of place!" She took a magnet that was half an inch, and put it onto the door. The door immediately collapsed.

The door led to the kitchen area, where they sat around the table. "Where should we look first for the lost furniture and stuff?" Pyro asked Thorn. "Not sure. But, we'll have to check any room that's open. No unlocking a door. We wouldn't want to attract unwanted attention."

A little girl ran into the kitchen singing a song.

"*I know someone will rescue me. I guess I'll have to wait but deep, deep down I start to drown because I know my fate. No one can remember me and now I'm all alone with nothing to call home. Just me, myself, and I, just left alone to die.*"

She began to sob.

Camilia felt bad for the poor girl. But more importantly, where did she come from? Camilia looked at Pyro, and Pyro looked at Thorn. Thorn signaled for Camilia to go talk to the little girl. They noticed she was half-frog, half-human, like Scat.

Camilia confronted the girl and asked why she was so upset.

The girl looked at her with trusting eyes and stammered, "M… my meanie uncle, Scat, locks me in the basement every day and never lets me out. So I don't have friends. I managed to escape and I just want food, but I'm afraid he'll find me!"

"My name is Camilia. What's your name, sweetie? And why does your uncle trap you in the basement?" Camilia said quietly, wanting to befriend the girl.

"Call me Tad. Uncle locks me in the basement because he says I distract him from his work too much and I'm a disappointment. Right now he's trying to attack every human in a local high school and get them to fight against all reptiles so that amphibians will rule the island and soon the planet! But what do I know?" Camilia introduced Tad to Thorn and Pyro as they left the building. "Who's your friend?" Geck asked, meeting up with her friends near the bushes.

"This is Tad. She's Scat's niece. But don't worry, she's not evil like him. Tad is going to help us learn more about the case of the missing teachers," Camilia stated.

"What about the South team's belongings?" Geck asked. "We'll have to figure everything out later."

"So what else can you tell us about the missing teachers?" asked Camilia as they were about to leave.

"Well, I know that the teachers are being kidnapped, but I don't know where they are. They should be somewhere around the temple," Tad replied as she twirled around in her pretty pink gown and caressed her curly orange hair.

"Do you know who's capturing them?" Thorn asked.

"My cousin, Iguan. She and Scat's army are taking teachers so parents and students will want them back, but they will have no choice but to bow down to them to get the teachers back!"

Iguan hopped down from the tree that she was watching them from.

"Iguan, what are you doing here?" Camilia asked, very annoyed.

They got out their weapons and then Iguan exclaimed, "Wait! I don't want to fight you, especially not you, Thorn." She winked at him.

"What is your problem?" Camilia asked, pushing Thorn back slightly.

"I'm here to deliver this scroll," Iguan explained, taking a dusty rolled up paper out of her backpack. Thorn eyed the scroll carefully. "Who's it from?" he asked. "I can't say," Iguan replied stubbornly, "But, if you come with me, I can tell you..."

Thorn smirked and took the scroll. "You're very delusional," he said. "That's what makes me single," Iguan joked. Thorn opened up the scroll and read it carefully. Geck nearly pounced on him, trying to see what it said. Thorn pushed her off his back and explained, "It's a silent manuscript. You can only understand if you're the one reading it.

"Give it!" Geck commanded, holding her hand out. Thorn shoved it at her forcefully. She snatched it from him and read. Then, she gave the scroll to Camilia. Camilia read the scroll and handed it to Pyro.

Pyro read the scroll and handed it back to Thorn. "Thanks, Iguan. Now leave," Camilia said angrily. "Could I at least ask what my cousin's doing here?" She replied. "I'm going to be a hero!" Tad sneered. Iguan turned, ready to run off. Then, she replied, "Tad, I'm warning you. Don't hang around the Reptiles. They're trouble."

After Tad told the Reptiles everything she knew about the missing teachers, they let her go to her cabin in the forest.

Before she left, she turned to Camilia and said, "Camilia, please don't go back to Scat's temple. He's a bad Amphibian man!"

Camilia smiled at the child and replied, "Don't worry about us, Tad. We'll be okay. Be safe in those woods." Tad nodded and ran off.

The next morning, Geck was at her locker getting her books for the first class period. She looked exhausted. Once she closed her locker, she was surprised to find Mr. Tony, the science teacher, behind her locker door, giving her an eerie-looking grin.

"Good morning, Mr. Tony," Geck said with a nervous tone in her voice.

Mr. Tony snapped out of his gaze and said, "Oh. Good morning, Geckeliette. I just wanted to make sure you were alright. You look a bit tired."

"Tired? Well kind of. I was up all night…studying," Geck said.

Geck had to lie to him because she knew that Mr. Tony was very suspicious about Thorn, Camilia, Pyro, her, and the whole Reptile clan. Geck also knew that if any Natural, or human, found out the real reason that her team was gone most of the time, it could start a war.

On the first day of school, the Reptiles met up at a cafeteria table and discussed how they could put a stop to the Amphibians from terrorizing villages and the school. Mr. Tony, who was nearby, overheard this. He'd been keeping an eye on them for a long time.

Mr. Tony gave Geck a grimace. Then he replied, "If you say

so…" He walked away, looking at her out of the corner of his eye.

Geck wiped her forehead as if she was to say, "That was a close one."

Then suddenly a hand grabbed her hand and pulled her into the janitor's closet. The door was shut behind her. To her surprise, it was Camilia. "Watch it! You could've got us caught!" she scolded.

"I don't appreciate being spied on," Geck snapped, flipping her ponytail sassily, "And could you remind me why this whole Amphibian thing is so private? It's more work trying to keep this secret than to be on the actual team."

Camilia put one hand on her hip and replied, "Everyone, besides you, Thorn, Pyro, and me, are Naturals. Do you really think we can trust them?" Geck opened the door slightly, observing all of the humans. They looked…different. They had eyes with small pupils, peach and brown skin. No green scales, no tails, and only 20 something teeth.

Looking back at her friend, who had green scales and a chameleon tail, she sighed. "I suppose not. But, do we have to keep this secret for the rest of our lives?"

"Listen, we've been getting more updates from the South team about the missing teachers. Right now, we can take a break while they take over the mission," said Camilia, intentionally avoiding her question.

In science class, the whole class got shivers up their spines as Mr. Tony slowly walked into the classroom. As he did, half of the class started gossiping and whispering to each other.

"I heard he killed like three of his ex-girlfriends."

"Don't be silly, he can't even get one girlfriend."

"I heard that he's a spy, secretly working for terrorists."

"Good morning, class," he said, sharpening his pencil with a cutting blade. "Today we will learn about atoms, protons, and neutrons."

CHAPTER 4

MR. TONY AND MS. CLOVER

Meanwhile Thorn and Pyro had a mixed math class. In mixed math class, some freshmen and sophomores had class in one classroom.

Everyone loved Ms. Clover, the teacher who spoke with a thick Irish accent.

Thorn, who was reviewing his textbook, noticed something strange about the classroom. Normally, the trash bin was empty, but now it was flooded with papers, crumpled up into balls.

"Class, today we will be taking a pop quiz. I hope you've been paying attention during algebra."

Pyro was not paying attention. He just stared at the clock above the chalkboard, wondering when the agony of boredom would end. Today was different, though. He stared for a different reason. It was not because of boredom, but because of him. Pyro felt unusually tired today. And when he became tired, sensibility slipped from his mind.

Pyro just hoped he wouldn't burn anything with his…powers.

"Class dismissed," said Mr. Tony. Everyone left, staring at him out of the corners of their eyes. He asked Camilia and Geck to stay. The two girls looked at each other and shivered, but they sat.

To break the awkward silence, Camilia mumbled "Y…you wanted to see us Mr. Tony?"

"Oh yes, that's right!" He nearly shouted. He made the two girls quail. "Now tell me, what were you really doing last night? Why don't you sit down next to me and we'll chat. Scoot closer to me."

Camilia and Geck scooted their chairs up until they were in front of his desk. Mr. Tony discussed what Geck had told him earlier. "Mr. Tony, I don't believe we have any upcoming tests. I have no idea why Geck would be studying for…"

"Geckeliette, would you mind telling me why you were studying?"

Geck looked down and mumbled, "I guess I didn't…realize. All I know was that I was studying."

Mr. Tony chuckled, seeing the guilty expression on her face, "Do you think I'm some kind of ignoramus?"

Camilia sat up straight and cleared her throat. She replied nervously, "No, of course not. Mr. Tony, our next class is starting soon. Could you please excuse us?" Mr. Tony stood up immediately and responded, "You mutants are full of lies! You don't think I know about all of the teachers that have 'left the school,' right?" Geck stood as well, making sure they made eye contact. Then, she said, "So, you think I'm a liar, huh? Well, let me just tell you that not every word we speak is your business. We may be just students, but we are students at this school!"

Mr. Tony adjusted his tie and opened the door. "Follow me," he said, holding back a snicker. Camilia stood up and followed him and Geck out of the room.

"Alright, class dismissed. Have a nice day, everyone!" Ms. Clover gleefully proclaimed. All of the students rushed out of the room; all except for Thorn and Pyro. Ms. Clover left to copy some papers.

"Why are we still here?" Pyro asked, pulling his hoodie sleeves over his hands. Thorn walked towards Ms. Clover's desk and signaled for Pyro to follow him. "This garbage can. This garbage can is the reason why," Thorn replied, pointing at the bin he saw earlier. "Look, Thorn, if you want to talk…" Pyro began, wondering what Thorn was doing.

Thorn crouched down and opened one of the cabinets. "More

paper balls," he muttered, picking up one of them. "It's a note." Pyro did the same and told him, "Yeah, it's several notes!" Pyro read over it and gasped, dropping the paper onto the ground. "This is the language that was on the scroll Iguan gave us, the scroll that you can't read out loud!"

Thorn quickly stuck the paper into his satchel. "Yes. We'll probably need this for later," Thorn answered, closing the cabinet and standing back up.

Ms. Clover walked in the room, mystified by the two students behind her desk. "What in the world are you doing still in here? I never would've thought teenagers would stay in math class longer than they're supposed to!" she chuckled. Pyro laughed along, trying to make everything seem natural.

Thorn took one of the notes out of the trashcan and handed it to Ms. Clover. "Ms. Clover, could you explain this?" Ms. Clover dropped her clipboard in fear. "Oh, dear," she muttered under her breath, backing away. "You boys...have to go." "Ms. Clover, are you ok? We just want to know how this ended up in here," Pyro tried to calm her down.

Ms. Clover sat down, sweating bullets. "Get out," she commanded. Thorn cleared his throat and told her, "Ms. Clover, who is this from?" "Get out!" she repeated herself angrily. Thorn placed the paper back in his satchel and nodded. He left the room, with Pyro following behind.

Mr. Tony, Camilia and Geck marched into Ms. Clover's room to see her with her head down on her desk. "Ms. Clover, is it alright if I speak to you about these mutants...or students?"

Ms. Clover sighed and nodded, putting her head back up. "Mr. Tony, I need to discuss something with you first," she said, motioning towards the corner of the room. Mr. Tony followed Ms. Clover behind a large cabinet. "Martin, a mutant found out," Ms. Clover sighed, shaking her head in disbelief of what she just said.

Mr. Tony's smirk turned into a scowl, "What are you saying, woman?"

"A mutant found out! Two of them found out about the notes!" Ms. Clover insisted. Mr. Tony placed his palm on his forehead. "How could you let this happen, Jewel?" he asked, feeling very irritated.

Camilia and Geck began talking about what was going on. "Do you think we're in trouble?" Camilia asked Geck. "I know we are," Geck replied, "But, the worst thing they could do is yell or give us a detention."

"A detention?! I've never gotten one in my life. I'd die in detention! I'm trying to keep a perfect record!" Camilia cried, "I don't even know what we did wrong!" Geck patted her on the back and said, "Hey, don't worry. We might not. Mr. Tony is just being weird, like always. We probably won't get in trouble."

Mr. Tony and Ms. Clover confronted the two mutant girls. "You can go," Mr. Tony said to both of them.

Meanwhile, at the temple, Scat's wife, Scurry, was making his dinner. Scat was in his throne chair, reading the newspaper. "Local village destroyed? Yes, that's us!" Scat happily said to himself, when Iguan stormed through the door. "I've delivered your scroll, daddy. The Reptiles are now in a state of confusion. I believe we can manipulate them to following our command," Iguan informed her father, bowing in respect.

"Good girl, Iguan. Do you have any questions on this mission?" Scat asked proudly.

Iguan looked at him and said, "Daddy, why are we terrorizing the North school campus? Don't we have better places to destroy?"

Scat cut her off, "You know what? My plan is so brilliant, there is no question that could possibly be asked! Have you gained those rotten Reptiles' trust yet?"

Iguan looked a little offended. "Not yet, daddy."

"Oh! I apologize, my princess! I meant that team, not the species," Scat said sincerely.

And then Iguan looked up at him and responded, "Okay, Daddy. It's alright. I won't bother you anymore. But answer this question. It's obvious that Mom didn't give birth to me. I want to know where I come from. Was I adopted? Was I an orphan?"

Scat looked shocked. "What do you mean? Is this really important to you?"

Iguan then got up and stared her father in the eyes. "It is. You are an Amphibian species. I am a Reptilian species. How are we even related?"

Scurry ran out of the kitchen with a bunch of maids to see if he would dare try to answer that question. Why was she the only Reptile while the maids, butlers, guards, and her parents were all Amphibians?

"I knew this time would come. You'd become curious. Well, a long time ago," Scat explained, "there was a war between Reptiles and Amphibians. The Reptiles won every battle until the very last year of fighting and violence. I was a young man back then, about in my early 20s, when I was forced into war by general Long Leap, your grandfather. Eventually, two of the Reptiles married," Scat expounded.

"The wife had a beautiful daughter. But during the war, the Amphibians had so many losses, that we decided to take drastic measures. One day I was sent to destroy the Reptile hideout. In the hideout, I placed a bomb. Before I left, I saw an adorable little baby. It wasn't in my heart to leave an unattended infant to explode, even if it was a Reptile. So I took the baby and raised her. We won the war as soon as the child turned 8 years of age and learned how to handle weapons. It was the rise of the temple. Nine years later, here you are. My princess…"

"Wait, so you like, stole me?" Iguan asked. Curiosity and confusion wrestled around inside of her brain.

"Calm down, Iguan. You were in danger! If I didn't save you, you wouldn't be here today."

"Yeah, well if you didn't try to blow up our hideout, maybe I could've lived with my real family and my kind would've won! You cheaters! We never tried to destroy your hideout. The Reptiles fought for justice and righteousness! You fought out of jealousy or greed!" Iguan ran to her room with a feeling of betrayal and loneliness.

Her mother followed her. "Sweetheart, it's not like that!" she called out before she could slam the door.

"Oh, are you saying that Amphibians are better?" Scurry looked around and said nothing. Iguan became furious as all the Amphibian workers watched in the background.

"Reptiles rule! And if dad, I mean if that's what I'm supposed to call him, really cared about that 'poor adorable baby' then he probably wouldn't have made me believe otherwise. Maybe he could've given me to my real parents or some other Reptile! I'm not one of you and I never will be! And I never heard of this until now? Why did you make me turn against my own kind, my real family?"

When her teary-eyed mother stared at her, she closed the door in disgust. Scurry covered her face and ran towards her husband.

"What do we do now? We have made our own child turn against us. You should have never told her. I would rather have Iguan be happy than know the truth!"

The devastated frog-woman, Scurry, ran into the kitchen with her three mutant maids following her and trying to comfort her. Scat was upset as well, but he knew Iguan would find out eventually.

Back at the school, the Team Reptilian was in their hideout at the basement of the school. Thorn was on his laptop deciding the best time to sneak out to the temple later.

Then Camilia and Geck ran in. Pyro, who was on the couch

watching Zombie Skull Crushers101, said, "Look who's late again."

"Well, we were late for a good reason this time," Geck replied, "Mr. Tony wanted to talk to me and Camilia earlier. It was one of his theories that we're spies or some crap like that."

Camilia sat next to Thorn and said, "Then, he talked to Ms. Clover...and said we could leave." Thorn closed his laptop and responded, "It's cool. Pyro and I got here like a few minutes ago. We found these weird notes in Ms. Clover's classroom. You know the scroll that Iguan gave us earlier?"

"Yeah, so what?" Geck scoffed, twisting her ponytail in braids. "The notes were the same language. It's not understandable if read out loud!" Pyro stated. Camilia turned to Thorn and asked him, "So, where are we sneaking into tonight?"

"I was able to hack into the schedule system of the Amphibians. Apparently, nobody is on guard around 5:00 p.m. We'll leave in an hour," Thorn explained.

An hour later, The Reptiles arrived at the temple.

"Why are we in our school uniforms?" Camilia asked.

"We have to be in disguise if we want to rescue the teachers," Thorn said.

"Why do we need to disguise?" Pyro questioned.

"Well, maybe it's because we're secret agents, not 'hey everyone, look at us,' agents." Geck mumbled, rolling her eyes, "So, who's going in?"

Thorn gave Geck his satchel and said, "Slice it."

"Slice what?" Geck asked nervously. "Anything that moves. Good luck," Thorn replied, giving her a dagger. Camilia tilted her head towards Pyro slightly. Thorn noticed this and let out a big sigh and mentioned, "Take Pyro with you."

CHAPTER 5

BREAK IN

Pyro almost choked on his own revelation. "Are you serious? I get to do something again? Great! So, what can I do?" he asked eagerly. Geck stood up and held her hand out for Pyro. "You can do anything I tell you to," she replied. Pyro gripped her hand, letting her pull him up. "And what do you get to do?" he asked. "I get to tell you what to do. Now, come on! It's not going to be 5:00 p.m. forever!" Geck teased.

"Camilia and I will be protecting the doors. Both of you don't attract any attention. Remember, when the wind blows against the tree, its leaves can only land on the ground."

Pyro nodded dutifully and replied, "I don't know what the last part means, but I won't say a word."

Geck tugged Pyro's sleeve, letting him know that she wanted to go inside the temple. Pyro obeyed her and followed her inside.

Pyro and Geck saw no security at the front door of the temple. "What time is it now?" Pyro asked. Geck checked her watch and said, "It looks like 5:10 p.m., should we go in?" Pyro gave her thumbs down. "The place is probably packed. If the guards aren't outside, then they're definitely inside. In the *Zombie Sneak Attack 2 Manual*, every good adventurer knows that you must find a secret entrance. If we can't find one, we make one!" "And if it's a hole, I push you down it?" Geck yawned.

Pyro scanned the area, and observed a large hole in the ground. "How'd you know it was a hole?" Pyro asked. Geck turned and noticed the strange void in the dirt. "I didn't, but do you think it leads to the temple?" Geck pondered. Pyro shrugged, reaching down to see how deep it was. "Let's check it out," he replied, climbing down the pit. Geck waited for him to see if he'd come back up.

Camilia stood in front of the main door, waiting for Pyro and Geck to return. "Maybe I should've gone along," she thought to herself, "but I'm sure they'll be alright." Camilia, overwhelmed with curiosity, peeked inside of the building. There, she witnessed a throne carved out of solid gold.

"This must be the lobby. I bet Scat is rich," she supposed. She opened the door a bit wider, until she felt a tap on her shoulder. Turning around, she realized it was Iguan. "Iguan?" she muttered.

Iguan, who was visibly displeased, said, "Camilia, what are you doing here?" Camilia wasn't sure what to say, and her mouth was moving faster than her brain. She replied, "I'm just…hanging out." "Hanging out in front of Scat's temple?" Camilia nodded. "I don't believe you. Tell me what you're doing here, now!" Iguan replied stubbornly.

Camilia turned away from Iguan and said, "Nothing. Just, go away!" Iguan whipped her katana sword out of her belt. "Tell me, or leave!" Camilia crossed her arms and protested, "Why are you even here?" Iguan chuckled smugly, "You stupid Reptile. I live here! Now, leave."

Camilia shook her head and said, "I'm not stupid! Go inside. I dare you." Iguan lowered her eyebrows and smiled deviously.

Thorn watched quietly behind an apple tree. Two Amphibians were talking about Scat's latest scheme. "I hear he's restocking all his weaponry," one gossiped. "Yes, he's really focused. Pretty soon, all the teachers in that dumb high school will be eliminated! The Reptiles will surrender once we get to the students!" the other replied.

Thorn processed the information in his head carefully. "So, the Amphibians are…killing teachers?" he thought to himself. Both Amphibians went inside, allowing Thorn to follow them in. "Wait, explain the plan to me one more time," one of them said to the other.

"Scat is kidnapping the teachers at Forestry Evergreen High. If the Reptiles don't surrender after we kidnap a certain amount of teachers, we just kill 'em off," the other explained. "Soon, we'll get to kidnapping students. If the Reptiles still don't do anything about it, we blow up the school!"

"Why do we want the Reptiles to surrender?" the first Amphibian questioned.

"That way, we can make a truce with them. Then, they can't stop Scat from taking over the island. Maybe even all of Phenise! He'll be unstoppable!" the second gushed.

They walked into a room and shut the door.

"Pyro, do you see anything down there?" Geck asked, poking her head down into the hole. She didn't hear a clear response, just a muffled voice. "Pyro, are you okay?" her voice echoed through the vacuum of the deep burrow. She heard nothing except her own voice repeating back. Geck was tired of waiting. The inquisitiveness was getting to her head. "Pyro, I'm coming!" she hollered, jumping after him.

In the hole, it was dark and silent. The quietness rang in her ears. "Pyro, this better not be a joke!" she cried, startled by her own loud voice. Geck tried climbing back up, but was brought down by an avalanche of soil. She coughed out all the dirt and covered her eyes. The last thing she saw before being crushed by a swarm of pebbles was a golden, glowing light.

Camilia flipped her hair gracefully. "Go ahead! Get in the building!" she commanded. "Look, tell me why you're here, and I'll leave you alone," Iguan promised.

Camilia looked at the ground with guilt and admitted, "All right. I'm here because...Thorn is looking for you." Iguan giggled mockingly, "Thorn? How could Thorn be looking for me? You're crazy." "But it's true!" Camilia insisted. He wants to ask you out. He didn't want me to tell you, though."

Iguan gave Camilia a look that could drop a bird from the sky and spoke, "Is that so? Why should I even trust you, Reptile?" Camilia generously placed her hand on Iguan's shoulder and said, "Because we're sisters, technically. Maybe...maybe you are a Reptile, but you're just working for the wrong team. Thorn knows that you're good, but he won't like you until you show him that you are. Did you ever think of that?"

Whenever anyone said the word *Reptile*, it made her think of her past. It made her think to herself, "Why do I feel like that word defines me, but it doesn't describe me?"

Not this time, though. Iguan could now think for herself. After years of being brainwashed, she could finally think as clearly as she could see. "Camilia, I've heard enough lies. I'm not stupid anymore. If you want to break into the temple or something, fine. Just don't go in my room, okay?"

Camilia had nothing more to say. Iguan got in her truck and drove off.

In the room, the two Amphibian men placed their knives in a briefcase and closed it, and locked it with a key. "I can't wait for Scat's master plan to occur!" The first laughed. The second put his coat in the closet and replied, "I am excited as well, brother, but we have to keep our voices down. I sense the presence of a third shadow in this area."

Thorn sat quietly in the closet, buried knee-deep in black briefcases. "What are all these briefcases doing here?" Thorn mumbled, but not loud enough for anyone in the room to hear. The two Amphibians were onto him. He needed to go and escape or stay and fight. Either way, he needed a plan.

"I heard rattling in our closet!" the Amphibian, Void, mentioned. "I hear it too. Get the daggers out of the case," the other one, Charcoal, agreed.

Charcoal slowly opened the closet, to see no one there and angrily growled, "Bloody nonsense, I know I heard a sound!"

Before he could turn his body to leave, a piercing sensation impaled Charcoal's back, not too far from his neck. The pain dragged him down to the floor. "Ah!" he yelped, falling onto his knees.

Void stared in horror at his friend, visibly shocked and confused. "Ch...Charcoal?" he stuttered, very disturbed, "Dude, what the hell happened?!" Charcoal was too overwhelmed with pain to even utter a word.

Void's soul was burning with the feeling of grief. He needed to avenge his friend. "Who did that? Come out, coward! Come out!" he shrieked, pulling his blade out of his pocket, scanning his surroundings. A second later, he was pounced on and pulled down to the floor along with his dying friend. Trapped in a headlock, he looked up to see it was Thorn. "Reptile, please release me!" Void cried.

Thorn snatched the blade out of Void's hand and threw it across the room. Then, he released him and helped him up. "You, what's your name?" he asked. "Void! It's Void! Don't hurt me!" Void pleaded, backing away from Thorn.

"I'm not going to hurt you yet..." Thorn said mischievously. "Sit down." Void did what he said without a second of doubt. But the entire time, he gazed at his unconscious teammate with hurt in his eyes.

"Tell me all about Scat's strategy, and don't try to lie, because I've heard most of it already." Void covered his face, ashamed of his tears. He wanted to say something, but he didn't know what to say.

Geck's eyes opened and the light was now closer, and the heat became a relief from the cold of the underground soil. "Geck? Geck, wake up!" she heard Pyro's voice. Looking straight ahead, she saw Pyro, crouched down beside her. "Pyro..." she mumbled, catching her breath.

"Geck, I found the entrance!" he gushed, reaching his hand out to help her up. Geck gave him her hand, and they both stood. "I found the entrance to the temple. It's this way!" Geck followed him to a small window at the end of the tunnel. "Should we open it?" Geck asked. Pyro shook his head and replied, "It's not locked, but there are Amphibians in there. We should wait until they leave."

Waiting was one of Geck's least favorite words. Whenever she heard it, she felt like doing the opposite. "How many are in there?" she rolled her eyes. "Actually, just one," Pyro said, peering through the blurry window. "No problem! If you're too scared, I can take him!" Geck laughed, flipping the window lid open and sliding through. "Geck, stop!" Pyro snapped, but in a whispery voice.

Geck landed on her feet, but made a loud thumping sound in the process. Looking around, the room was flooded with cobwebs, filled with dark corners and turns, and dimed with the only lighting being shone from the two-foot square window at the top of the wall.

Ironically, the silence of the room was deafening. Not even the whirling winds outside could be heard through the open window. "Pyro, do you mind?" she asked, looking up at him through the small window. Pyro put his arm through the window, and it glowed a lava filled orange color.

The room turned brighter, but not crystal clear. Every time Geck took a step, the dust from the concrete floor would roll off her shoe and into the air. "This room must be really old," she said quietly. "Pyro, are you coming down or what?"

Pyro shook his head in disagreement and said, "No way! I am not in the mood for lung cancer!" Geck was ready to climb back up and rip out his lungs, but that's when she heard the rattling. "Who's there? Hello? Come out and fight me!" she warned, removing her rapier sword from her satchel.

The rattling grew louder, coming from one of the many dark corners.

Thorn was growing impatient. "Well, come on!" he growled at Void. Void cleared his throat and replied, "Reptile, there is nothing more. You've heard our plan already. Please help my friend! I will pay you handsomely."

The guilt grew bitter inside of Thorn, but he tried to ignore his feelings. "Tell me where the teachers are hidden."

"I was told that they are kept in our basement!" Void coughed out of weakness.

Thorn nodded and gave Void his scarf to wipe up the blood. "Take care of your friend," he said, leaving.

Geck strode slowly towards the nearest dark corner; where she found a man in a black trench coat digging through a large crate viciously. "Where is it?" he muttered, "It has to be in here!" Geck was confused. Was the man speaking to himself? A sense of fear rushed through her veins, but she did it anyway.

"Sir, are you…" she began, tapping his shoulder. The man, who was an Amphibian, lost his mind and threw her into another corner. "Ow!" she whined. Pyro saw her being thrown against the wall and quickly jumped down the window chute.

The man's face was covered by a ski mask and he was 7 feet tall. He angrily charged towards Geck, who was too paralyzed with fear to move an inch. Pyro, without second thoughts, gripped on to the man's trench coat and tried to pull him back.

The man growled like a wild bear after hibernation and pushed Pyro onto the cemented ground.

Camilia gazed down the large hole in the ground. "What's going on down there?" She wondered. "I have no idea," Thorn replied out loud, causing Camilia to nearly fall down it. "What are you doing here?" Camilia asked, blushing slightly. Thorn pointed at the small chasm. "I spoke to one of the Amphibians. He told me that the teachers should be down there."

Camilia scratched her head and replied, "It sounds like a bear attack down there! Wait, you don't think Pyro and Geck are..."

Thorn jumped down the warren before Camilia could finish. "Join me," he said, reaching his hand to her. Camilia sighed, acknowledging that this was a bad idea, and let him pull her into the ground. They found the window a second later. "In here," he whispered, slipping quietly through the window.

The bloodcurdling figure in the trench coat swept Geck off of her feet and left the room, locking the door without even stopping. Pyro got up and dusted himself off. "He got away!" Pyro said, noticing Thorn and Camilia entering.

Camilia twisted the doorknob repeatedly, but it wouldn't budge. "Locked," she said. Thorn opened the window as wide as he could and insisted, "You guys wait in the van."

Before he could climb out, Camilia gripped onto his arm and scolded, "No you won't! We're going to come with you! Thorn, you can't go and face that guy all by yourself. It's risky!" "So am I," he interrupted, "And I know what I'm doing. Trust me."

Camilia and Pyro followed him out, and then entered the van. Thorn entered through the main door without hesitation. No one was there but him. It was like the entire temple was empty. Thorn quickly took out the scroll that Iguan gave him. "This scroll...it must be a map."

He opened it and proceeded to a smaller door behind a staircase. There, he found Geck. She didn't move; she just laid there, eyes open, but barely breathing.

"Geck," Thorn mumbled, grabbing her by the wrist. Her pulse was fine. And to his relief, she blinked.

Thorn soon noticed the ripped up clothes. The stitches on her hoodie were all torn-up. The seams of cloth on her sleeve were shredded. Even the heels of her sneakers had holes in them. Her hair was now messy and tangled.

"This was no ordinary mutant," Thorn sighed, "It must've

been a Superfluous mutant." Geck's curiosity came right before her well-being. "A Superfluous mutant?" Thorn nodded, and picked her up like a child awake in its crib. "What's a Superfluous mutant?" she asked, yawning peacefully. Thorn didn't respond, but he carried her back to the van. He placed her on the front passenger's seat.

Camilia brought her a blanket and wrapped it around their young friend. "What happened to her?" Pyro asked, hovering over her seat. "Is she going to be okay?"

"She's just resting, Pyro. Thorn, where did you find her?" Camilia asked. Thorn gave Camilia the scroll and replied, "She was under a staircase for some reason."

CHAPTER 6

WHEN SHE HIT THE GROUND

"What about the teachers?" Pyro questioned. "We'll return," Camilia responded. "If the staff discovers that we've been gone for so long, we'll surely get in trouble."

All week, Geck wasn't her usual fierce, bold, and independent self. Her self-esteem was lowered so much; it was even more devastating to watch the young girl slowly die inside. All confidence she had was violently knocked out of her when she hit the ground that night. Now, she could barely stand by herself without questioning it.

Geck was too confused for any educational subjects, too sick for lunch, and she never got any sleep. She was too tired for anything else. In art class, she would always paint a slender, black shadow onto her paper on the easel. This was odd for her art teacher, because Geck was one of the most creative students in the school.

The poor child could ponder nothing but that horrible thought. That beast called the Superfluous mutant was ruining her life, socially and personally. The school nurse and the school counselor explored this peculiar behavior, but had no clue of what was going on.

One day, Geck was at her locker, upset, and getting her books. Her gecko eyes were pink from crying so much, she had bags under them. The girl was tired, very tired.

Then, Diane and a group of preppy kids confronted her shamelessly. Diane walked up to Geck and mocked her, "Why, look everyone! It's Geck the wreck!" All of Diane's popular friends chuckled snobbishly.

"What's wrong Geck? Realize that you can't get a date unless you legally change your name?" The popular kids behind her laughed.

Geck didn't verbally reply. She just pictured the beast that carried her away, taunting her with similar insults as he threw her onto the cold ground. "Say, I'd ask you to be my science fair partner, but I think you'd make a better science fair project! Speaking of an experiment gone wrong, what's this nightmare?" Diane giggled; snatching Geck's painting from her, "Gross, it's wet! Did your dog throw this up?"

Geck had enough. Slamming her locker door, she turned around and took a deep breath. "I created it! Creation is something you probably wouldn't understand because you just destroy everything you see!" she scolded her.

Geck wanted to throw her onto the floor just as the Superfluous mutant did to her, but no one, not even her bitterest enemy, should know the pain she felt when she hit the ground. Even facing hundreds over other pet peeves in the cafeteria felt better. That's where she was heading.

Then, Geck bumped into Pyro. "Watch where you're..." she didn't have the courage to finish harassing him. Pyro, who was waiting for an insult, was quiet as well. But, breaking the silence he asked, "Geck, can we talk?"

The two of them sat at a lunch table not really making eye contact. Then Pyro spoke. "What really happened in the temple earlier? You know, when that Superfluous mutant kidnapped you?" He said it so suddenly, it made Geck gasp in fear.

And then Geck quietly responded, "Actually, I'd prefer not to talk about it."

"C'mon! You could tell me!" Pyro said.

Geck shook her head and replied, "No, I can't. The things that

Amphibian did to me were just…I don't want to talk about it."

Pyro, trying to hide his shock, said calmly, "Well, that's okay. Just, think of anything you want to tell the beast and say it to me."

"Are you sure?" Geck sniffed bashfully. "I wouldn't want to hurt you the way I want to hurt that monster."

"Just pretend that I'm your…emotional punching bag. Verbally abuse me as much as you want, and I won't be affected, because I know you're not speaking directly to me. Go ahead, try it. It'll make you feel better."

"That's the worst part! If you were the beast, I'd be running away screaming and calling myself a coward," Geck sulked hopelessly, looking down at her feet. Pyro lifted up her chin gently and smiled, "Don't tell yourself that. Lying isn't right."

Geck hated when he made her blush, but she allowed it this time. "Thanks, Pyro, but that's not going to help me get over this. I'm slowly going insane, and not even the strictest mental asylum can help my case. No one can help me."

Pyro shrugged and said, "Maybe it's because you're not letting anyone. Instead of thinking about your one weak spot, think about your million strong points. I think about them all the time, and so do Thorn and Camilia. That's why we're your friends." Geck wiped away one of her tears and walked off, thinking about what her friend told her.

Camilia, Geck, and Mishell went over to the mall to shop for clothes the next day. Camilia and Mishell were hoping that this would make their grieving friend forget about her sadness. As soon as they opened the door, humans were staring them down like chickens entering a butcher store.

To add to the awkwardness, a mall cop ran up to them in shock and said, "Hey, are you three real Reptilian mutants?" Each one of them looked at each other, and nodded at him. "I've never seen any up close!" the man exclaimed. "I've always wondered about what happened to make you people half reptile! Do any of you know?"

"I don't know, we were just born like this, I guess," replied Camilia.

"How does it feel to have green scales and tails?" asked the policeman.

Geck, who was getting fed up, tried to defend her race, "I don't know! How does it feel to have a white skin and an…"

"What she means is," Camilia tried to rephrase, "that we are just like people, even if we look a little different."

"Is it true that your people jumped in toxic acid just to get attention?" The policeman continued, not taking a hint.

"No, that's silly!" said Mishell.

Geck was rolling up her sleeves and cracking her knuckles. The policeman chuckled and said, "I heard that America was so embarrassed by you freaks that they kicked you out of the country!"

"I heard that America was so lazy, that they couldn't even rebuild their land and that they relied on us 'freaks' to provide them a new home!" Geck almost yelled.

"Geck, that's enough!" Mishell mumbled through her teeth. Camilia yanked the two of them by the arm and dragged them out the door.

In the van, Camilia and Mishell kept giving Geck dirty looks. Finally, Geck noticed and said sharply, "What?!"

"What was your problem back there?" Camilia scolded her.

"Yeah!" added Mishell. "That was so embarrassing!"

Geck just took out her journal and started to write. "It's not my fault! He was mocking us. Someone needed to speak up!" She tried to explain.

"You know our place! Our ancestors made a deal with the Naturals a long time ago. We were told by the government to treat the humans with respect, or they could take this country for themselves and ship us off again. The Naturals are always right!"

Camilia insisted.

"So what if Naturals have a little more power?" Geck argued. "They are respected so much that they basically already own this country! How is it fair that they forced our kind to come here, and when we finally get used to the conditions and adjust, they come in and steal our freedom? Hasn't anyone ever questioned this or tried to fight back? Hasn't anyone ever rebelled?"

"Geck!" Mishell interrupted, "Nobody has ever rebelled because nobody cares! The Naturals get their way, and that's that! You're not supposed to question it."

Geck just pouted. She didn't think it was fair. But the only thing that was more unfair was that nobody was doing anything about it.

Once they got back to the campus, nobody said a word.

It was Monday. The school hall was full of busy students and staff rushing to get to their classrooms.

Thorn was in Mr. Beasley's history class. "Okay, class," Mr. Beasley began, "Can anyone tell me why the Americans came to Phenise?"

A boy named Samuel raised his hand, "Acid spilled into the oceans and all the water went bad and became polluted, along with all the air. This caused America's population to plummet, and the government didn't want that."

"Correct. Any questions?" Nobody had their hand up except Thorn. "Thorn?" Mr. Beasley pointed at him.

"How come the Americans had to look for land instead of everyone just going their separate ways and immigrating to different countries in the world?" Thorn asked.

Mr. Beasley was not sure how to answer that. Throughout the 30 years he'd been teaching, nobody had ever asked him that.

"Well, that was a time period where America wasn't really in touch with all of the other countries, and the acid fumes and high explosive activity created low satellite signals and no access to other countries. Maybe, they were having trouble flying their planes?"

"Did you just tell me that in the form of a question?" Thorn replied.

"No! I meant, nobody is quite sure yet, but there are theories!"

"Okay, so basically everything you told me before is a lie, right?" Thorn asked.

"No, it's just my theory!"

"But, I didn't ask for your theory."

"Look, kid. I don't know!"

"Then, why did you answer?"

"Thorn, if you know so much, why don't you teach this class?"

"Because I don't have 30 years of experience and a degree in teaching."

"That's it, smart mouth. Do you want a detention?"

Thorn smirked deviously, "I just asked a question."

CHAPTER 7

THE TRUTH CONCEALED.

"Alright, Mr. Woodland, maybe you should keep your mouth shut and let me teach. After all, you are just an ignorant Reptile. You wouldn't know America's history as well as an American." Thorn didn't say anything, but his eyes indicated his thoughts. Mr. Beasley was acting unusually nervous.

All of the students started heading out, except Thorn, who was hiding behind a desk. He waited for everyone to leave, and for the teacher to turn off the lights and close the door, and then he got up. Thorn sauntered to the stack of papers on Mr. Beasley's desk and looked through the files.

Eventually, he found what he was looking for. A paper that had classified in red on the cover. Thorn opened it without second thoughts. Maybe it had something about the origin of the Reptiles in it. The bell rang again, which meant that it was time for the next class. Thorn grabbed his backpack and shoved the paper inside of it. Then he left, hoping nobody saw.

It was 5:00 p.m. and all classes had dismissed, meaning the students could change into their regular outfits and go out with friends or just stay in their dorms and relax. But not team Reptilian. They always met at the school basement after school.

Camilia, Pyro, and Geck were waiting impatiently for Thorn. "What's taking him so long this time?" asked Geck.

"Beat's me," Pyro said. "He always lectures us about being late, yet he's always the last one here!"

"Do you think he has a good excuse this time?" Camilia wondered out loud.

"I don't know. Maybe he is out in the woods with Iguan again!" Pyro teased her.

"Yeah, he has been talking about her a lot lately!" Geck added.

Camilia picked up her hairbrush and said, "Leave me alone, guys. Thorn will get here soon."

Just as she finished her sentence, Thorn entered, tossing his backpack across the table, almost hitting Pyro in the face. "Dude, why are you late?" Pyro nagged.

"Because I have an excuse this time," Thorn replied cunningly. He took the stack of paper out of his backpack and dropped it on the table.

"Ooh! What's this?" Geck asked, spectating at the papers.

"Well, have any of you guys ever wondered where we came from?" Thorn queried.

"Not really," Camilia retorted.

"Sometimes," Pyro sighed.

"All the time!" Geck replied.

"After class, I decided to do a little 'exploring' and I found this on top of Mr. Beasley's desk," Thorn explained.

"And you found these papers?" Geck questioned.

"Look on the back of this paper," Thorn said, and he took the paper on the bottom of the stack and brought it out. Geck flipped it over. It said, "History of the Mutants" on it.

"How did you find these?" Geck wondered out loud.

Thorn told his friends about what Mr. Beasley said, and how he couldn't answer his question.

"Wait, he called you a what?" Camilia asked in disgust.

"An ignorant Reptile," Thorn said, quoting his teacher.

"Racism at its finest!" cried Pyro.

"Did you tell Principal Lewis?" Geck questioned.

"No. Then, he'd do that cheesy thing where he makes people apologize to other people and he'd say his speech about how anti-bullying can solve world hunger and stop global warming. Besides, Sensei Sudoku told me, 'When being shot, do not lose too much blood or you shall die.'" Thorn said.

"Oh...and what does that mean?" Pyro asked.

"If someone tries to put you down, don't let it affect you too much, or it will haunt you for the rest of your days."

"That's kind of depressing," sighed Geck.

Thorn was about to flip open the first page, when his pager began to beep. He responded to it immediately. "The Amphibians are at Dirtstown again. They're taking more dwarf people captive."

"My pager says that they got there an hour ago," Pyro said.

"One hour ago? I just got the signal now," Thorn said, checking his pager again.

"Maybe there's a really weak connection or something. I heard rumors of the Amphibians hacking the connection system from us to the paging tower," Pyro informed them.

Everyone stared at him. "What?" he uttered.

"How come you didn't tell us?!" Geck scolded him.

"I didn't know if they were true!" Pyro yelled back.

"Where did you hear the rumors?" asked Thorn.

"I can't exactly remember..." Pyro said, squinting his eyes. He usually squints his eyes when he tries to focus. "I think that I heard it from Lizzy or something."

"Lizzy?!" the other three cried. "Out of all people, Lizzy knows this? Isn't she retarded or something?!" Geck asked, slightly upset.

"Geck, you say *mentally challenged*, not *retarded*," Camilia corrected her.

Geck put her hand on her forehead. "There's going to be a lot of ninjas at that village," she said quietly.

"How would you know that?" asked Pyro.

"Why wouldn't there be? Maybe the Amphibians finally learned from their mistakes. They probably decided to bring a backup," Geck insisted.

The team got in the van and drove to the South school campus to receive help from their fellow Reptiles.

They arrived at the South Campus. In the van, everybody was arguing about who had to knock first.

"In my opinion, Thorn should go first since he's the leader!" Geck said.

"I think that Pyro should go, because he's the reason why we're here!" Camilia scoffed.

"I'll go," Thorn said, and got up.

"I'll come along," Camilia responded.

"Me too!" said Pyro.

"I want to come!" Geck replied.

Thorn gave them looks that could dent the roof of a truck. "I'll go," he said once more, leaving the vehicle behind.

He knocked on the door, and it fell down. Behind the fallen door, he saw Scales kneeling down with a hot glue gun and hammer. "Hi, Thorn!" Scales smiled broadly. Thorn waved slightly, a bit confused about the dark ring around his right eye.

"I was just fixing this door. The Amphibians destroyed it when they broke in and took everything," Scales replied, leaving to get more nails to fix the door.

Thorn entered and looked around. Lizzy and Mishell rushed to the door. "Good evening, Thorn!" Lizzy beamed. "Have any of you seen Repto?" Thorn asked.

"He stepped out to fix the pager signals on the roof. The pagers have been malfunctioning, lately," Mishell corrected. Thorn handed Mishell his pager.

"You know, our systems have been monitoring weak connections towards you guys. Do you still receive any crime alerts?" Mishell asked, studying the pager carefully.

"Yeah, but the one we recently received is one hour late. We're going to need backup to stop the invasion of Dirtstown," Thorn explained.

"Right now? You can't stay for a cup of tea?" Lizzy mumbled.

"People are being burnt as we speak," Thorn mentioned.

"Then let's go!" Scales said, running out of the door.

They arrived to see thousands of ninjas attacking helpless villagers. "Those poor people!" Lizzy cried.

"Okay, Camilia and Scales, you two go hack the system of the ninja base. Pyro and Mishell, you guys find the mayor and get as many citizens as you can to a safe place. Lizzy, Geck, and I will go over to the temple and find out what's causing the late connections to our pagers. Let's move!" Thorn commanded everyone.

Everybody rushed to their positions immediately.

CHAPTER 8

SEVERAL PLANS, ONE GOAL

Mishell and Pyro searched the town for the mayor, despite all of the chaos going on. A burning building on every street, corpses lay on the dirt, motionless, and broken glass was stepped on with every inch they moved. They both cringed at everything they saw.

The two stopped looking once they saw a little girl with green skin and a ninja wrestling over her purse. Mishell carried the girl away from the man while Pyro snatched the purse from him. They gave it back to the girl. "Oh, bless both of you!" she cried. "Is there a way I can repay you?"

Pyro knelt on one knee to make direct contact with her face. He soon realized that the girl was Tad! "Tad, have you seen the mayor anywhere?"

"Yes, Mr. Pyro. I saw him go into that cave over there!" Tad said, pointing to the cave behind her. Pyro picked her up and went into the cave. Mishell followed.

Camilia and Scales climbed onto a van entirely covered in leaves and sticks. Inside the van, a sign read, "Property of the Amphibians." "Wow, I wonder whose van this is," Scales muttered sarcastically.

"Wait a minute," Camilia said, "There are thousands of ninjas in the village. How did they all fit in this van?" Scales looked around, then pulled a curtain from the door.

"Maybe this helped?" Scales asked. A gigantic box had a huge label on it that read, "Cloning device".

"Wait a minute. The Amphibians have been cloning themselves this entire time?" Scales asked.

"I guess so. But that's not important right now. We have to mess with all of the pagers off each ninja, so they'll think that Scat is telling them to retreat!"

"That's a genius idea!" Scales agreed, "Except we don't know how to do that."

At the temple, Thorn, Geck, and Lizzy stood in front of the large door. "So, what's the plan?" Lizzy asked, looking at Thorn.

Thorn thought for a moment and then replied, "We open the door, get to the control room, shut off the security cameras, and interrogate an Amphibian about the cell towers."

"What if there are Amphibians behind the door?" Geck questioned.

"Then we'll go through the back," Thorn replied.

Mishell, Pyro, and Tad were now going through the cave. Pyro was using his torch hand to provide light for them. Occasionally, they heard eerie wolf-like noises, but they tried to ignore them.

Eventually, Mishell decided to start up a conversation. "So, I wonder what those weird noises are."

"With today's school lunches, probably indigestion," Pyro replied.

"You're funny, Pyro. I wish Repto had the same sense of humor," Mishell mentioned randomly.

"What do you mean?" Pyro asked her.

"It's just...Repto and I started dating a while ago, and he's kind of boring. I mean, he's never cracked a joke or laughed at funny movies, or even smiled lately. He doesn't know how to have any fun," Mishell sighed.

"Maybe he does have a sense of humor, but his is just different from yours."

"And what do *you* mean?"

"I mean, everybody has a different type of funny bone. Some people like cheesy puns, some people like knock-knock jokes, and some people like complicated riddles and rhymes. As long as it makes you laugh, then it's what you consider funny," Pyro explained.

"Wow, that's really a...philosophical way to look at comedy!" Mishell laughed.

"Well, anything is possible if you make it philosophical," Pyro gushed. "You two are kind of dorks," Tad muttered, rolling her eyes.

Meanwhile, Scales and Camilia were looking at the control panel of the Amphibians' van. "Alright, I don't know too much about all this nerdy, computer, electronic stuff, so I'm just gonna watch for now," Camilia insisted.

Scales looked at her and shrugged, then continued studying the controls. "Are you sure?" he asked.

"Maybe you can tell me what everything is, then I could try?"

Scales was getting fed up with Camilia ruining his concentration. "Fine. There's a red wire, a blue wire, and a green wire. A red one, a blue one, and a green one, okay?" he stated.

Camilia just nodded, and then she noticed him squinting. "You're squinting! You're just like your brother!"

"No, I'm not..." Scales mumbled.

"I'm sorry, am I bothering you?"

"No, it's just...I had a rough day at school, okay?"

Camilia touched Scales by the shoulder tenderly. "Yeah, so?" she mocked him.

"It's just. The older kids kept on making fun of me today. They always do, but it was really bad today."

"I'm sure you're overreacting," Camilia interrupted him.

Scales turned and looked up at her. Camilia gasped, turned bright yellow, and covered her mouth in horror. They gave him a black eye! "Scales, oh my God! Your right eye is...!"

"I know, I know, it looks bad, but I'm fine...really!"

"Why didn't you tell a teacher?"

"Because, the older guys told me that if I spoke a word to any of the teachers, I'd get one on my other eye!"

"Scales, this is terrible! You know you could've defended yourself!"

"Yeah, but fighting them would make me just as bad!"

"Okay. Okay. How old were the boys?" Camilia asked, trying to calm down.

"Three were eighteen and one was nineteen, I think."

Camilia turned dark red. "Seniors did this to you?!"

"Camilia, please calm down! We have to get back to our mission! More yelling won't make me feel any better!" Scales cried, tearing up and using his arms to block his face.

"Alright. I'm sorry, Scales. You're right. I'll just watch."

Scales continued to study the wires.

At the temple, Thorn and Geck were both helping Lizzy climb through the window. She was surprisingly heavier than she looked, so Geck had to climb in first and pull her by the arms while Thorn was outside trying to push her through the window.

"Come on, Lizzy! Just put your leg over the wood!" Geck instructed.

"I'm sorry, but I can't! This is just too hard! I lack the energy!"

"And I lack patience, Lizzy. We're running out of time. If this pager isn't completely broken, it says that there are less than 100 villagers left," Thorn warned her. "Alright, I'll do it for the villagers!" she replied gallantly, forcing herself through the window. "I did it! I really did it!" she gushed. Geck patted her on the back and replied, "Yeah, and it only took 20 minutes!"

Thorn pointed towards the end of the hallway and said, "I see the control room. Let's go."

In the cave, Pyro, Mishell, and Tad were getting tired, and stopped and sat against a boulder to take a rest.

Tad took out her lunchbox from her pink backpack and grabbed her Peanut Butter and Jelly sandwiches. "Do you guys want some?" "Sure!" Pyro said, taking a sandwich. "I'm good, thank you," Mishell said politely. Out of nowhere, a moaning sound was heard. It sounded like an old man. "What was that?" Tad asked, gripping onto Mishell's arm.

Pyro picked up a stone and stood up, slowly moving towards the back of the rock. "Ms. Mishell, do you think that was a monster?" Tad whispered. "No sweetie, maybe it was just the wind," Mishell assured her. Then, they heard it again.

Back at the Amphibian team's van, Scales told Camilia everything to know about hacking into the pagers.

"Alright," Scales explained to Camilia, "Now, the red wire is connected to the blue wire. Got it?"

"Got it!" Camilia said eagerly.

"Good. The blue wire is the wire that triggers the green wire, okay?"

"Okay!"

"The green wire is usually triggered by the red wire, but in this case the green wire is connected to the blue which is connected to the red, so it's not, right?"

"Um...right!"

"The blue wire can't be cut until you get rid of the red wire, or the pagers of the ninjas self-destruct and kill them. Are you following me?"

"Well, uh..."

"And the red wire sits on top of the blue wire, so you must move the red wire next to the other green wire, not the first one, or that one explodes too, cool?"

"I...don't understand..."

"Yes, you do. Now, there's actually a black wire. I just told you there are three colors to make sure you were listening. Were you?"

"Wait...what?!"

"I know you were. Basically, don't touch the red wire until it gets behind the black wire, or the black wire electrocutes you. If it's behind the blue wire that absorbs all the energy, then it short circuits, making it okay to touch, therefore cut. That will cut the power from each pager and reset all the data, so we can use our pagers to hack the messages. Understand?"

"What are you talking about?!"

"Excellent, you're catching on! Now you try!" He smiled, handing the small, metal pair of tweezers to her. Camilia gulped. She was just confused by an eight year old.

Thorn, Mishell, and Lizzy were at the front door of the temple's control room. "How are we going to get in now?" Lizzy asked, trying to turn the door knob of the locked door. "Say that a little louder, Lizzy," Thorn told her, thinking of an idea.

"I said, 'How are we going to get in now?'!" Lizzy hollered. Footsteps rang to the beat of her echo. Thorn signaled to Geck and Lizzy, telling them to hide behind the corner. A maid named Claire paced from the opposite side of the hall, to the door.

"Hello? Who's there?" She was holding a dagger and walking around the area. Thorn sneaked up behind her with a rag, knocked the dagger out of her hand, and covered her face with the rag, pulling her towards the ground.

After struggling, screaming, and panting, she finally calmed down. Lizzy and Geck looked down at her. "Thorn, I don't think she's breathing," Geck supposed. "Is she dead?" Lizzy asked, fear in her eyes.

"Of course not, Lizzy. She's just taking a 'surprise nap,'" Thorn assured her. He lifted her body up and balanced her torso over his shoulder.

Once they got in the van, the maid woke up, rubbing her head. Thorn removed the rag from her face. Once the maid woke up and she saw Thorn, Lizzy, and Geck all staring at her as she shrieked helplessly and fell to the floor. She covered her hands and cried,

"Please don't tell my boss! He'll kill me if he finds out that I've been kidnapped!"

"Hey chick, you know where we could find a control room around here?" Geck began to interrogate her.

"Control...room?" she stammered quietly.

"Don't play dumb, blondie!" Geck threatened her. Thorn put his finger to his mouth as if telling her to be quiet.

"Alright, what is your name?" Thorn asked.

"Claire Morphus."

"Who do you work for?"

"The almighty master, Scat."

"Why?"

"Because he is the almighty master, Scat."

"Do you know everything about your master?"

"Yes."

"No you don't. I bet you don't know where his pager control room is," Thorn teased.

"Yes I do! I know everything! Ask me where it is."

"Where is his pager control room?"

"Third door to the left down the hall!"

Claire quickly covered her mouth, regretting telling him.

Lizzy was writing down all of the information in a notebook. "Okay, we can't release her until we fix the connection signals," Thorn told the two girls. "We'll have to move swiftly. There's probably more of her kind guarding that door."

In the cave, Pyro was getting ready to throw the rock, but then he saw an old man lying on the floor, tears in his eyes, and dirt smeared everywhere on his body. Pyro put the rock down immediately and tapped Mishell on the shoulder. Mishell turned around and gasped. She got up and ran to examine the old man.

He had a hat that read "Mayor" on it. "Sir, are you alright?" Mishell whispered to the man.

"You...the Reptiles! You...you are too late! All of my people, gone! They...they are all dead! There is no one to save! G...go home!" he yelled at them.

Tad crawled in front of the mayor and patted him on the head. "There, there, Mr. Mayor. It's not too late! The Reptiles came right on time! There are still people they can save, right guys?" Tad asked, looking up at Pyro and Mishell. They both looked at each other and shrugged. "I don't know, Tad," Pyro said sincerely.

"Uncle Scat wouldn't go as far as to destroy a village just to get the humans on his side, would he?" she asked them.

"Everything will be fine, Tad," Mishell assured her. But she wasn't even sure herself.

Camilia was sweating cataracts. She was so nervous about moving the wrong one. Scales was becoming impatient. "Okay...uh... what did you say about the red wire again?" she asked.

"Camilia, I respect that you like to take your time, but we kinda have to hack the Amphibians' pagers today!"

"You're putting pressure on me!" Camilia cried, reaching for the black wire.

"No! Don't touch that one!" Scales screamed, pushing her out of the way.

He was instantly electrocuted. He collapsed onto the carpeted floor. "Scales!" Camilia shrieked and picked him up. "Oh no! You poor thing!" Her pager began to beep. It said, "Insert message here".

Camilia put Scales down. She had five seconds to type the message to the Amphibians' pagers before each of their pagers blew up. But she didn't care. It was a Reptilian tradition to serve the mutant who risked his or her life for you if they survived. She needed to get him to safety.

In the village, more dead bodies than before were either impaled into walls, hung on trees, or lying down in burning buildings. The Amphibian ninjas were high-fiving each other and cheering for themselves. "Our first village, completely destroyed!" one of them said. "Yes, now back to the van," another one said.

Then, the leader, Gallant, adjusted his mask and said, "Scat will be so proud of me. But wait, I hear something. Weapons, obtain!" Every ninja got out their nunchucks. They heard footsteps coming from a cave. Each group of ninjas approached the inside slowly and quietly. Gallant signaled for the other groups to stay outside, while he and his two other men went inside.

Gallant and his men were walking at a tiptoeing pace.

Gallant then saw it was Tad. "Hey little girl, you're our boss's niece, aren't you?!" Tad crossed her arms and said, "What do you jerks want now?!"

"Stupid child! Don't you know your place is with us?"

"If my place is burning houses and killing people for sport, then I don't want my place!"

Mishell grabbed Tad by the hand and whispered, "C'mon, sweetheart. Don't talk to these troublesome boys. Let's just finish eating our lunch and leave with the nice mayor."

"Did I hear someone say mayor?" Gallant asked nosily, pacing around Mishell, observing her features.

"None of your business," Mishell scolded him. "Who do you ruffians think you are anyway?"

"I can't speak for those two, but they call me Gallant. And they must call you, gorgeous," Gallant said, trying to flirt with her. Mishell blushed and pushed Tad behind her. "Listen, I don't know what you Amphibian menaces want, but just leave us alone! You've already stolen from an entire colony. What could you possibly want to take from us?" she scolded.

Gallant walked up to Mishell until they were face to face. "Maybe...a life or two?"

Tad was so nervous, she found herself screaming at the top of her lungs. "Mr. Pyro!" Pyro, who was trying to stitch up the mayor, heard his name, and sprung to his feet directly. "There's a guy scaring us!" Tad called out to Pyro.

Pyro turned around, squinted, and saw Gallant and his posse. He confronted them and meekly asked, "Can we help you dudes?"

Gallant stared Pyro straight in the face and said, "So, is this your girlfriend?"

"What? No!"

"You wouldn't mind if me and her went somewhere?"

"No! I mean…yes! I would mind!"

"So, she *is* your girlfriend?"

"No, she's not."

"Then what's with all this jealousy?" Gallant mocked him, and grabbed Mishell by the waist.

Mishell shrieked fearfully. "Let go of me!"

"I'm not jealous! Please, just let go of her. I don't want to fight you!"

"What if I do this?" Gallant asked stubbornly. He stuck a pocket blade in Mishell's mouth. She continued to gasp for air.

"Seriously, let go of her!"

"Why, because you're jealous?"

"No! She already has a boyfriend!"

That finally got through Gallant's head, and he stopped arguing. "Let go of Ms. Mishell!" Tad yelled at him, kicking Gallant in the shin. "Very funny, child," he snickered, pushing her off.

"I don't see her boyfriend…" he said.

"Yeah, that's because he's not here!" Pyro insisted.

"Really, where is he?"

"Somewhere else…" Pyro mumbled, flames glowing in his veins.

Gallant backed away slowly. "An Ignitodile?" he mumbled. "Never thought I'd live to see one."

Pyro calmed down instantly, acknowledging what Gallant had just said. "Look, you should just go," he recommended quietly.

Mishell, terrified, spit the knife out and pushed Tad even farther back. Tad, on the other hand, was amazed. To her, Pyro was like some cool dragon guy.

Gallant and his boys felt intimidated, but they wanted to come with them, and they weren't leaving without a fight.

CHAPTER 9

FALLING APART

Camilia didn't know where to go. Scales lay unconscious in her arms, her pager had no signal and she was completely lost in the base of her worst enemies. Worst of all, she heard footsteps coming towards the RV.

"The door is open? I thought we locked it!" Camilia heard a voice say. A series of confused murmurs followed. Camilia flung Scales behind the large, brown box and hid with him.

Four ninjas jumped onto the RV. One of them got out a remote and zapped the other ninjas outside. They all vanished. The door was shut. Another one of them sat in the driver's seat and started the engine.

"What a day!" The third one said, collapsing on the couch, "I'm exhausted!" "Do you think we should wait for Gallant?" the fourth asked the first. "Nah," the first replied, "He'll catch up."

The RV drove off, with Camilia and Scales inside it. The four ninjas were just chatting amongst themselves and relaxing. Meanwhile, Camilia was about to have a panic attack. But, she calmed down and prayed that Scales would wake up once they got to the temple. Fortunately, his eyes opened.

Thorn, Lizzy, and Geck were in front of the security base of the pager controls door.

Thorn placed his hands on the doorknob. An alarm went off. It sounded throughout the temple. The clanking of rushing boots boomed throughout the hallways.

"Okay. I think there's a trap door through this entrance!" Geck theorized.

"You think? Geck, this isn't a guessing game. We can't afford anymore false alarms," Thorn warned her. They heard the sound of guns being loaded coming closer.

"Just trust me!" Geck yelled at them. She opened the door. Thorn shrugged, covered his eyes, and went through the door. Geck followed, and Lizzy went along.

"I'm not leaving without this chick," Gallant insisted. "Yes, you are! And she's not a chick, she's a girl!" Pyro exclaimed.

Gallant ignored him and tugged on Mishell's hair viciously. "Cut it out!" she cried.

"Mr. Pyro, do something! He's hurting Mishell!" Tad told him. Pyro looked at his kunai dagger and up at Gallant.

Pyro ran his fingertips over the dagger object and sliced Gallant on the jaw. Gallant dropped Mishell and touched his face in shock. Blood dripped onto his hand rapidly, Pyro didn't enjoy drawing blood, but when he did, it was to protect others.

Mishell ran behind Pyro and clutched onto his waist in fear.

"Pyro..." Gallant mumbled, taking out his katana. "Now it's my turn..."

"What happened?" Scales asked Camilia, wiping the drool off of his face. "Quiet down, Scales. Everything will be fine," Camilia tried to convince him.

"I heard a voice," a ninja named Dusty said. He stopped the RV.

"It's coming from behind the box!" another one named Dart pointed out.

The other two ninjas walked towards the box and removed it. Camilia looked up with fear. Scales, unaware of what was happening, got up and stretched as if he'd just woken up from a deep slumber on a Saturday afternoon.

Dusty and Dart did not say anything, but just stared at the two in disgust. Scales blinked twice and then looked up to see the two ninjas eyeballing him. He quickly ran behind Camilia and hid.

Trying not to make things too awkward, Camilia spoke. "Wow… this isn't the bathroom?" she mumbled.

"Halt!" one of the ninjas yelled at her, aiming his shotgun. "State your business, petty Reptiles!"

Camilia stood right away and put her hands up. "We surrender." Scales got up as well, "No we don't!"

After hours, Thorn, Lizzy, and Geck woke up in a dark room. It was pitch black and empty. Thorn pulled out a box of matches from his pocket. He lit them immediately, and the room grew bright.

"What happened?" asked Geck, rubbing her head.

"You should know. You dragged us down here!" Lizzy said in an annoyed tone.

"I saved our lives!" Geck argued, getting up on her feet. Suddenly, the lights turned on. Ninjas with their rifles were lined up by the hundreds against each wall.

"Our hero…" Thorn rolled his eyes.

"Listen, if you stop the vehicle and let us leave, we can forget all about this!" Camilia assured them. The RV stopped. The other two ninjas crowded around the scene.

"You Reptiles are so pathetic that I almost want to let you go. But the boss wouldn't like that," Dusty laughed. Another ninja, named Rusty, whispered in Dart's ear. The fourth, Don, smirked.

Dart grabbed Camilia by the arm and sat her down on the couch. "Is this your friend?" He asked her. Camilia did not reply. "Be like that…" he muttered under his breath.

Rusty gripped Scales on the shoulder and lifted him up. "W… where are you taking me?" he questioned him, very afraid.

Rusty opened the door and lifted Scales higher. "No!" Camilia shouted, getting up right away.

"Zip it sweet cheeks, or you're next!" the other ninja, named Snipes, scolded her. Camilia pushed him out of the way. "Don't you

CHELCIE C. OPARANOZIE

75

let go of him!" Camilia warned Rusty.

"Oops!" Rusty smirked, dropping Scales out the door.

The door shut and Dusty started driving. "Oh no…" Camilia sputtered.

Pyro and Mishell continued to defend Tad from the other Amphibians.

"This girl belongs to us!" Gallant roared, slicing off a piece of Pyro's sleeve with his katana.

"She belongs to Repto!" Pyro corrected him, piercing Gallant's shoe with his dagger. Gallant used his blood-stained foot to kick Pyro onto the dirt.

"Pyro!" Mishell shrieked. She ran next to him and knelt down. "Are you alright?!"

"I'm…look out!" Mishell ducked. One of the men swung his sword right over her head.

"What are you doing?!" Gallant nearly shrieked, "Don't kill the girl! She's what we're trying to get!"

Gallant was enraged when he saw Mishell hugging Pyro and crying. "Oh, Pyro, please don't risk your life for me!"

"Dude, I'm not risking my life," Pyro smirked, "This guy couldn't hurt me if I had one leg!"

"Is that a challenge?" Gallant smiled. He pushed Mishell off of him and stabbed Pyro in the knee. Blood flowed to his ankles speedily.

Pyro got up, limping. "Is that all you've got?!" He yelled at Gallant fearlessly, secretly wishing that it *was* all he had.

"So, you think you're pretty tough, yeah?" Gallant chuckled, pulling out his Wakizashi Sword. "Boys, head back to the RV. Let's see how 'tough guy' fights with no legs!"

"Hey, that's not playing fair!" Tad said, sprinting at him and latching on to his leg.

Gallant giggled and then kicked Tad against the rock. She was knocked out instantly. "This isn't a game, fool!" He laughed and aimed the sword at Pyro's other leg.

Pyro fell to the ground weakly. Gallant was ready to swing, but then felt pity for him. "Can I have the lady now?"

"N...never!" Pyro replied stubbornly. Gallant raised his sword in the air.

Then, he felt a warm hand grab his wrist. His wrist was heating up. The hand was burning him! The sword melted right out of his hand! "Ah!" he yelped, shaking the hot metal off of his burnt fingers, "You burnt me!"

"Let's see how well you fight with one hand!" Pyro mocked him, picking his Kunai dagger back up.

"You know what? I don't even need to fight you, flame freak!" Gallant speared Pyro on his palm, swept Mishell off the ground and into his arms. Pyro fell down once again.

"Put me down right this instant, you hooligan!" Mishell retorted, turning away from him.

"Don't worry. I'll put you down, alright," Gallant grinned, giving her a wet smooch on the cheek. He laughed triumphantly and stormed out of the cave with her.

Pyro just lay there, helpless, hurt, and mad at himself. He could've done more. But from time to time, he liked to forget that he was an Ignitodile, and pretend that he had no powers. Now, the only thing he could do was attempt to reach for his kunai, 20 feet away.

Thorn, Lizzy and Geck were completely surrounded by guards. "What now?" Lizzy mumbled to Geck.

"I don't know, Lizzy. But I think we might be able to..."

"Geck, this is life and death. We have to stop thinking and act fast!" Thorn rushed her.

Geck was never one to believe in 'no win' situations, but Thorn was right, like always. Suddenly, they heard a shriek. Thorn and

Geck turned to see Lizzy being dragged away by two ninjas. "Lizzy!" Geck cried, ready to dart towards the ninjas with her bow and arrow. Thorn grabbed her arm and shook his head as if to say *let her be.*

Two other ninjas grabbed Thorn by the arm. "Thorn! You can fight them off!" Geck shouted.

"It's okay, Geck. We're outnumbered. Just do what they tell you." They took Thorn and Lizzy outside to the execution table.

"Thorn! Lizzy! No!" Geck cried. "This is my fault! Me and my stupid head! All I do is think, but I never know anything!"

One tall soldier approached her. "The Master would like to see you." Geck knew exactly who "The Master" was, and she didn't want to see him.

The soldier pushed Geck into a 3-foot dog cage and locked it. Geck had to crouch down to fit inside it. The soldier carried the cage into Scat's room and left, locking the door.

Scat took off his hood and got up from the bed. He opened the cage. Geck crawled out like an animal. "Why, look here! They bought me a dog!" Scat chuckled. Geck stood up instantly after that comment.

"What do you want, Scat?

"I want your brain!" he said, getting right to the point.

"My brain?"

"Geckeliette, you have the intelligence of a Greek god."

"What do you mean? You want my brain?"

"You don't understand, child. You see, you have a power more special than any other."

"I do? What's the power? What are you saying?!"

"Will you let me finish?!" Scat snapped.

Geck was silenced. "Now, this may seem shocking to you, but I've had my scientists observe you for some time now. They've noticed how your actions reflect your thoughts. We have determined this special ability you have is…predicting the future."

"Rubbish," Geck spat.

"You must be psychic! You know what's going to happen hours before it does!"

"I didn't know you'd drag me in here and tell me I'm magical out of nowhere? Besides, why should I believe you?"

"Geckeliette, your powers aren't stable yet. You are not old enough to control yourself. But I am. Together, you and I can destroy your friends together!"

"You want me to kill my friends? The same friends that I've known and fought beside for years? Double rubbish!" Geck retorted.

"I know it doesn't make sense to you now, but it will. It's for the best," Scat insisted.

"Scat, we all know that you're a selfish, dirty frog that wants to have everything for himself, but I didn't know you were part rat too! Asking me to betray my own panel? Nice try, old man," Geck laughed in his face.

"Child, you know the world, but you do not know yourself! Think about what I say!"

"I have, and that's why I'm saying no," she tried to calm herself, "Now if you'll excuse me, I have friends to save."

Geck left the room. Outside, the sounds of booing filled her ears. "What's going on…?" she began to question…and then her eyes were saturated with fear. There, she saw Thorn and Lizzy approaching the execution table.

Camilia watched in horror as Dusty stepped on the gas pedal. Scales did not know his way back to his school. He was sure to get lost. "Please, you have to stop this vehicle! Drop me off too!" Camilia cried.

"Oh we will…in our dungeon!" Rusty laughed.

Camilia's one fear that she'd had ever since she was a little girl was to be kidnapped. Not only had she been kidnapped several times before as a child, but Camilia hated not knowing where she was headed.

"I said…stop!" Camilia threw her ninja star at Dusty. It sliced him on the back of his neck. Dusty fell to the floor. Blood sprung from his head.

"Ow!" he screamed, rolling around in pain. The RV hit a few bumps, and then tipped over the edge of the road. It was going out of control.

The other ninjas ran back and forth. Rusty tried to control the steering wheel, while Don and Dart tried to grab hold of Camilia. Camilia punched the glass of the window and threw the pieces of glass at them. They caved in along with Dusty. The vehicle, having dealt with enough pressure, tipped over. Camilia went flying to the roof of the inside of the car. She heard a cracking noise in her neck. Then she thrust herself out the door. With her luck, she plunged off the side of a steep crag.

Finally, her body came to a stop. Unharmed, besides the pain in her neck, she held on for dear life to the convenient branch dangling by the side of the cliff. Miles away from the ground, Camilia was absolutely helpless and dependent on the loose little twig.

The ninjas in the RV got up, dusting themselves off and picking the glass out of their slimy amphibian skin. "What the hell was that?" Dusty exclaimed, wiping the blood off his neck with a rag. "I don't know, brother. We must report to Scat," Dart insisted.

Don stood up and stretched. "That girl is crazy!" he thought aloud.

"We can't tell Scat. Surely we will be punished for letting one of the Reptiles escape," Rusty said.

"What now?" Dusty asked.

"We have to search for her and any other nearby Reptiles," Rusty insisted.

When Tad woke up, she saw Pyro laying on the ground in a puddle of lava. "Mr. Pyro!" She ran to him. "This is my entire fault!" She covered her face and began to weep. A tear drop fell onto Pyro's leg and he gasped for air.

"Ow!" Pyro moaned.

"Pyro, you're awake!" Tad yelled. "I'd hug you, but you look like road kill."

"Tad...where's Mishell?"

"Oh, I think they kidnapped her, but I was sleeping, so I don't know for sure."

"Okay, do you know where they might be taking her?"

"When my uncle usually sends out ninjas to kidnap people, he usually takes them to his dungeon below the basement. Sometimes when I slept at night I could hear their screams of pain."

"Okay...well I don't think that they're there. By the way Gallant was looking at Mishell, I think he wanted to hurt her himself."

"Listen, you have to stay here. I'm going to figure out where they're taking her...somehow."

Pyro struggled to get up, but his leg was still sore. "No, Pyro. This is my fault. I have to save her."

"How was this your fault?"

"Well..." Tad started, "I kind of...sort of...gave Uncle Scat the idea to attack Dirtstown, again."

"What?" Pyro said.

"Oh come on! The place is called Dirtstown! Who wouldn't want to take it off the map?"

Pyro glared at her with anger, scrunching his nose in fury. "Just listen!" Tad continued, "My uncle was stressing over the fact that you guys kept on winning every battle. The Amphibians try to distract you guys from all of the missing teacher drama. I told him that he should come back to this village with more ninjas."

CHAPTER 10

COLLAPSING

"Basically Mishell was kidnapped by a bunch of masked dudes, I'm slowly drowning in a puddle of my own boiling blood, Thorn, Lizzy, and Geck could be getting killed and you got kicked onto a rock all because you opened your mouth?" Pyro asked, not looking directly at her.

"Stop interrupting me! Now, he said that he'll think about it and he locked me in the basement again. I snuck out through a little window I found in the basement. It led to a hole in the ground. After I escaped, I came here, hoping I'd find you guys. And, I did! So, isn't it a happy ending after all?" Tad giggled.

Pyro was too disgusted to speak, and his eye-piercing stare implied it.

"I couldn't help it! I didn't think he'd actually listen to me! Besides, I wanted to see you guys again! I wanted to help!" Tad sighed.

"Tad, that's not the point! Everybody in this town is dead! That was really selfish of you!"

"You're making me feel bad!" Tad cried, putting her hands on her head.

Pyro calmed down. "Alright, as I said, I'll go look for Mishell. You stay here."

"But, your leg! You're limping!" the little frog girl reminded him.

Pyro got up and tried to maneuver. "Don't worry about me. I like a challenge," Pyro said, rubbing his leg gently, "Just worry about yourself. You shouldn't have much trouble doing *that*." Then he limped out of the cave, dragging his sword behind him.

"I have to help…" Tad mumbled. She quietly followed after him.

Back at the Northern School Campus, people were getting ready for the 100th Annual Freshman Dance on Saturday. Every year at the beginning of the school year, the school throws a dance for the freshmen, welcoming them into high school.

Students were asking each other out, student council was putting up flyers, and the School Beautification Club was hanging banners and handing out pins and bouquets of flowers.

Diana, on the other hand, wasn't focused on finding a date, or buying a dress, or even having a good time. She wanted to be the Freshmen Queen, even though she technically had to do all three of those things to win.

Diana and her main posse, Charlotte, Mia, and Amy, were discussing this at dinner. In Forestry Evergreen, people also ate dinner in the cafeteria. "I am so excited for the dance!" Mia shouted.

"Same!" gushed Charlotte.

"Me too!" exclaimed Amy.

"Girls, I'm excited too, but there's one particular topic I want to discuss," Diane interrupted, trying to sound professional, "And that is Freshmen Queen. Now that I…we are in high school, we have to show we're mature. I am not planning on doing any sabotage, but if you people don't vote for me, I'm not talking to you anymore."

"We're sorry, Diane!" all three of her goons cried in unison.

"Relax; I already know you'll vote for me. But, I just want to make it clear that I need your help for once."

"Our help?" Charlotte gasped, "What an honor!"

"Yeah, just make sure everyone votes for me, even if it involves money…" Diane warned them.

"But paying people to vote for you is against the rules!" Mia reminded her.

"No duh! Don't let any teachers know," Diane commanded

REPTILES VS AMPHIBIANS

them. The three girls saluted her.

"Now, I have some depressing news to share with all of you. Some idiots actually started voting for…Geckeliette."

Charlotte gasped. Amy shivered in revulsion. Mia gagged.

"I know, I know, it's disgusting, but every once in a while, stupid people are born. I guess 50% of them go to this school, because half of the school has voted for her."

"What? That's sickening!" Amy said.

"You three call Geckeliette and tell her to meet me in my dorm. If she doesn't answer, we'll have to go with drastic measures."

Charlotte, Mia, and Amy nodded and marched out of the cafeteria.

Lizzy was next in line for the Volt. The Volt was a machine that the Amphibians used to torture captives and trespassers. After you sit on the chair, you have to wait. A large axe-like tool will swoop down and slice off your head. The terrifying part is not knowing when it will happen. The axe can swoop down the second you sit, or it can take up to a day. It can take up to weeks or maybe even months. Waiting and starving is the most painful part.

An Amphibian grabbed Lizzy by the hand and threw her onto the chair. He blindfolded her and tied her wrists and ankles together.

Geck was outside, trying to contact the others on their pagers, but no one would pick up. "Dumb pager signal never works!" she shouted, throwing her pager on the ground.

"Maybe it's not too late. I guess I'll have to rescue them myself!" Geck ran back inside the execution hall. A huge crowd wearing all black was chanting, "Off with their heads! Off with their heads!" repeatedly. Then, she saw one of the executioners. She ran up behind the Amphibian, snatched the key from him and ran on stage.

The crowd of Amphibian people booed her, but all Geck was

focused on was saving her friends. She unchained Lizzy and Thorn from the handcuffs.

"To the van!" Thorn told them. After hurrying off stage, they made it safely to the van.

"Where to next, now that we failed?" asked Geck.

"Back to the village. Geck, page the others," Thorn instructed.

"I did!" Geck replied. "They didn't answer! I think that something might've happened to them!" Thorn didn't reply, but he just started the engine. "Scat told me something very interesting today!" Geck said.

Thorn snickered, "Okay then. What did Scat say?"

"He told me I have a special power!"

"The same guy who lives in a temple, sits on a throne all day, and kidnaps people for fun told you that you were magic?"

"No, he told me I was psychic," Geck corrected him. "Let's see how Pyro and Mishell are doing," Thorn retorted. They drove off.

After a while, they arrived at the burnt houses and blood-splattered corpses. "What happened? Where is everybody?" Lizzy asked.

"Hell," Thorn said grimly, "This town wasn't meant to last, anyway. The leader of this place is fifty and about the size of a yardstick. No one here could defend themselves."

"So, do you think Camilia and Scales found the team's vehicle?" Geck asked.

"Doubt it. But if they did, the ninjas probably went back to the temple by now."

Lizzy got out her phone. "I'll try and call Camilia." She dialed her number.

No one picked up. "That's odd. Camilia doesn't move an inch without her phone, and she definitely never turns it off!" Lizzy muttered.

Then Geck pulled hers out. "Maybe I could locate Camilia. She made me download this weird app that lets you track down your friends. I never really use it." She entered Camilia's number, "It's vibrating. It says keep going north."

Thorn, Lizzy, and Geck started heading north.

Pyro fell for the second time. He lost a bit of blood with every step. As his blood started to fade away, so did his courage. Could he really stand up to Gallant?

Then he got a phone call. He weakly picked it up from his pocket and answered. "H...hello?"

"Pyro, it's me!" A familiar voice came from the phone.

"Mishell?"

"Yeah! Where are you, Pyro?!"

"I'm...on my way...sort of."

"No! I just wanted to make sure you call an ambulance. You got hurt really bad!"

"It's not that big of a deal." He tried to get up, but he stumbled. "I'm fine. Don't worry about me! Where are you?"

"I won't tell you! I can find my way out!"

"Pyro! Please don't get involved. You've bled enough! Get help for yourself!"

Pyro paused. He was convinced that Mishell truly didn't want his help. "Fine. I won't come if I know that you're safe."

"You promise?"

"I promise. At least tell me where you are."

"Okay...I'm in the basement of the local jail cell of the town. It's dark and scary and..."

"Hello? Mishell, hello?"

The other line cut off. Pyro beheld all of the damage around him, including his leg. The only pain worse than the pain in his leg was pain in his heart. Everything in a once lively town, a once lively world, was dead. The only thing that could add to the suffering was knowing another person could get hurt, and letting it happen. "Why..." he mumbled out loud.

Thorn stopped in his tracks. "I heard a noise. Talking," he said. He took out his Falchion Sword. Geck and Lizzy tailed him as he sneaked behind a wall.

Pyro was about to proceed, but Tad started tugging his arm. "I told you not to come!" he scolded her.

"But I heard someone talking!" She grabbed him by the hand and pulled him behind a wall. Pyro pulled out his dagger.

"I heard footsteps!" Geck whispered.

"So did I!" Lizzy agreed. They took a step closer.

"Pyro, they're coming closer!" Tad muttered. They took a step closer.

Thorn and Pyro both raised their weapons and charged at the same time. They stopped as soon as they came face to face with each other. "Pyro?" Thorn gasped.

"Thorn?" Pyro said, baffled.

"What happened?" Thorn scolded him.

"I don't know! Mishell and I were going through the tunnel and we saw Tad and some old guy. We soon realized it was the mayor and I tried patching him up. Tad gave us sandwiches. They were really good. Anyway, Mishell got captured and I was on my way to find her. She's at the local jail."

"Pyro."

"Basically the reason why we're on this mission is because Tad told Scat her idea about destroying the town. I was mad, but I got over it. Basically, everyone's dead, but I'm just glad we found you guys."

"Pyro."

"So, did you guys get our Wi-Fi connection back? Never mind. More importantly, where are Camilia and Scales?"

"Pyro!" Thorn shouted.

"What?"

"Is Mishell okay?"

"I don't know."

"Where did you say she was?"

"A local jail."

"Who kidnapped her?"

"Some guy named Gallant."

"Is the mayor okay?"

"He's dead."

"Tad, what did you tell Scat?"

Tad scratched her head for a second. "Well, I remember telling him to send some ninjas here."

"Did you give him any more ideas on evil plots?"

"No, Mr. Thorn."

"Okay, then I suppose Scat's just lying around getting old. We need to find Mishell, then Camilia and Scales. Into the van, now," Thorn said.

Everybody got in the van, but nobody said a word for a while. Minutes passed, and Lizzy spoke, "When me and Repto were scared as kids, we'd always say a little prayer to reassure ourselves. Maybe we should try it?" Geck turned her head sharply and stabbed Lizzy with her eyes. Pyro, on the other hand, said, "I guess we can give it a shot. Why don't you start, Geck?"

Geck sighed and replied, "I would, but I think that Lizzy should start." Lizzy nodded and began to pray, "I pray that we make it to the jail safely." Tad joined in, "I pray that Ms. Mishell is alright and that my friends forgive me for what I have done." "I pray that the Amphibians will stop terrorizing villages," Pyro added. "I pray that they stop kidnapping our teachers," Geck admitted.

Thorn thought about saying something, but then they arrived at the jailhouse.

The van stopped in front of a gigantic old and abandoned building. "We can't afford to start anymore fights," Thorn said. "We have to sneak in, get Mishell, and leave. I'll go in. Pyro and Lizzy, follow.

Tad, whatever you do, do not leave this van. Understand?"

Tad sighed miserably. "Understood."

Thorn, Geck, Lizzy, and Pyro entered the huge, eerie-looking asylum. "Hello? Anyone? Congregation?" Geck called out.

"Quiet, Geck. We must stay hidden. Pyro, is your phone working?"

"I think…so," Pyro said. His skin was fading slightly.

"You don't look so good."

"Me? I'm…okay," Pyro tried to convince him.

Thorn took the phone from him and dialed Mishell's number.

"H…hello? Anyone there?" A scared girl asked.

"Mishell, it's me, Thorn. Are you alright?"

"I don't know. It's dark…and I'm tied to a chair!"

"We're in the building. Where are you?"

"No! I can't let you guys risk your lives for me! I'm fine!"

"Mishell, stop being difficult. You need our help!"

"No, I don't!"

Thorn heard a banging noise over the phone. "Mishell, what's going on?"

"The three boys are coming in."

"Who?"

"Thorn, I don't want anyone to get hurt!"

"What about you?"

She cut off. "She's not responding," Thorn said sternly, "This place is huge. We'll have to search the entire area. Pyro, where did you say she was?" "I…don't remember," Pyro yawned.

"Actually," Geck interrupted, "I think I might know where Mishell is…"

"Geck, please," Lizzy tried to stop her.

"My mind is telling me…Mishell is…right beneath us."

No one wanted to say anything to her. "Right beneath us?" Thorn asked. "Is this a sick joke?"

"No! No, it's not a joke! I can feel it!"

"Feel what? Feel the need for attention?" Lizzy asked, very cross-looking.

"I do *not* need attention from you people!" Geck yelled, "I'm just trying to help out!"

Pyro, feeling dizzy, tumbled onto his knees, and onto the ground. Lizzy cried. Thorn and Geck both helped him up. "Pyro, speak!" Thorn commanded. "I…was stabbed…" Pyro gasped weakly.

They soon realized that they were standing in a puddle of blood. "Oh my God!" Geck shrieked, "Pyro, who did this?! Why didn't you say anything?!"

"The…ninjas that…" Before he could finish, his eyes shut. Thorn felt Pyro's wrist. "He's out cold. Lizzy, get him back to the van."

Lizzy picked him up and carried him like a child. "Geck, tell me more about this 'thought' of yours," Thorn said to Geck.

CHAPTER 11

REVIVING

"I feel a...vibe," Geck told him. "The vibe tells me...there is...a basement. Mishell...she is inside of the basement. The basement is underground. Mishell is underground. Underground is right beneath us. Mishell is right beneath...us!"

"I suppose that makes sense," Thorn mumbled.

Lizzy came running in. "Tad says she'll help Pyro."

"Good. Now, let's check the basement. Mishell is in there alone with those guys. We must use caution." Thorn and Lizzy followed Geck to the basement.

In the basement, Gallant was untying Mishell from the cold metal chair. "Why do I feel so, weak...and numb?" Mishell asked him.

"My boys and I injected you with a poison that weakens your muscles, that way you can't escape. Or maybe it's because of how hot I am!" he snickered.

"Gallant, please! Let me go! Trust me, I'm not your type, but maybe we can be friends!"

"Quiet, sugarplum, or you're not going to enjoy this." He smirked and tugged her hair again.

"Ow!" she yelped, "What are you going to do to me?" "I'm going to ask you a few questions. It'll be fun, like a game!" "A...a game?" Mishell replied. "Yes, a game," Gallant snapped and his two muscular goons entered.

"You're not intimidating me!" Mishell scolded them. "Tell me where the Northern Campus of your school is located, baby," "As if! You must already know. Weren't you the one that was kidnapping teachers from that part of the school?" Gallant didn't talk. He snapped his fingers. The two larger Amphibians nearly ripped Mishell's hair off with their bare hands. "Ouch! Stop that!"

"Oh, I'm so scared!"

But when he turned around, he regretted his words. All of the ninjas on the Amphibian team knew Thorn, the guy that nearly killed their master with one throw. "Hey, Thorn, what's happening?" Gallant chuckled.

Mishell wiggled around in her chair, but she couldn't escape. "Thorn! I told you not to come and get me! I can handle these guys on my own!"

"Then why are you tied to a chair?" Thorn asked, walking towards her.

"I don't know," Mishell admitted, blushing.

Gallant untied Mishell carefully and said, "Hey, man, you know I was just playing around, right?" Thorn grabbed Mishell by the hand and helped her up. "You nearly sliced my friend's leg off," he replied. "You know, Thorn, you're lucky Scat isn't here. You would've been in his decapitation device as soon as you came in!" Gallant uttered. "Who asked you, Amphibian?" Mishell spat at him. Gallant shot Mishell a devious smile from the other side of the room. "Just because I can't touch you doesn't mean I can't watch you," he mouthed.

Thorn was walking back to the van, carrying Mishell on his back. "Why can't you walk, again?"

"Gallant and his thugs poisoned me, so now my muscles are numb for the next few hours."

"Cool. Have you learned your lesson?" Thorn asked. Mishell nodded, "Next time I'll ask for help when I really need it." "Yuck, you sound like a cheesy Christmas special," Thorn laughed. Mishell agreed and laughed with him.

They arrived at the van. Thorn placed Mishell on the couch.

"How's Pyro?" Thorn asked Tad.

"He's doing much better, Mr. Thorn! I disinfected the wound, stitched him up, and gave him a lollipop!"

"Good. Where is he?"

"Oh, he's just..." She looked around.

"He got off to use the restroom at a near gas station, I believe. He said he'll catch up with us," Tad tried to convince them.

"Pyro has a limp leg and is carrying a heavy gear belt and he's supposed to catch up with a Ford transit moving at high speed?"

"That's what he told me!"

Thorn raised an eyebrow and went back to his seat. "Yeah, I think we're going to wait for him."

"No!" Tad screamed. Everyone in the vehicle turned and stared at her. "No...Pyro said he doesn't want to waste our time. He says we should leave without him."

"I'll call him," Geck said, getting out her phone. "That boy takes forever in the washroom. You keep an eye on her." Mishell nodded, and Tad smiled, handing Mishell a lollipop.

Thorn, Lizzy, and Geck hoped off of the van. They soon witnessed a damaged, upside-down vehicle. The windows were shattered, the wheels were busted, the windshield was about 15 feet away from the van, smog was bursting from the wrecked engine, and the foul scent of gasoline spread throughout the woods. "Nice..." Thorn scowled at the smashed vehicle.

"Guys! Guys!" Scales ran over to them. "I thought I'd never see you again!" He leaped into Thorn's arms.

"Scales, what happened? Why is this thing tipped over?" Thorn asked.

"I have no idea. The ninjas dropped me off in the middle of these woods and I got lost."

"Do you know where Camilia is?"

"Nope," Scales said.

Thorn put Scales down.

"Wait a second," Geck said, "I think I still have that 'Pal Patrol' app that Camilia made me download. It helps you track your friends' phones."

Geck mumbled a few words and then read her phone screen. "It says that Camilia is…in a river?"

"In a river?" Thorn, Lizzy, and Scales echoed.

"That's what it says!" Geck insisted.

"There's a river off the edge of that cliff," Scales mentioned, pointing down at a faraway valley.

"Why would Camilia be in a river off a cliff?" Lizzy asked.

"I didn't see anything after they left me out in the woods," Scales said.

The others followed Scales to the rim of the bluff. "Who's jumping first?" Thorn asked.

"Ooh! I want to!" Scales exclaimed. He gave Lizzy his satchel and looked at Thorn for approval. Thorn nodded.

Scales jumped. "Are you crazy?!" Lizzy shouted at Thorn.

"I'm not the one who jumped off the cliff," he answered. Then he threw his grappling hook right at Scales' head. Luckily, Scales grabbed onto the rope. The sharp end of the hook darted into the rock. Scales safely slid from the side of the rock to the ground.

"Who's next?" Thorn gave Geck and Lizzy an evil smirk.

"Looks like fun!" Geck giggled. She strapped her satchel tightly to her torso. She leaned over and let herself fall off the cliff. Geck also grabbed onto the rope and slid down.

Lizzy looked down at the deep drop. "I don't know. I don't really like heights…"

"And I don't like you, but here I am," Thorn replied, loosening the rope. "You go first!" Lizzy pouted.

"I would, but then you'd have to slide down with the rope

unattached."

Lizzy began to shiver. "Can't you go without me?"

"There are still ninjas patrolling the area. Do you really want to stay here alone?"

"I want to go down, but what if I don't grab the rope?"

"Then, you just hope you live. That way you can learn from your mistake and do it right next time," Thorn insisted.

Lizzy gave Thorn her satchel. "I am afraid, Thorn. Will you go with me?" Lizzy asked, grabbing him by the arm.

"As Sensei Sudoku always said, 'When the falcon falls, it has most likely been shot,'" Thorn uttered. He unattached the rope. Lizzy just assumed that it was a 'yes.'

"Oh, and could you kind of go slowly?" she asked patiently, "I get queasy." She took off her glasses and placed them in the bag.

"You can't control gravity," Thorn told her, "But gravity can control you."

He tied the rope around both of them and grabbed on. Thorn backed away from the cliff. "Ready?" He looked at Lizzy. Lizzy nodded, tightening the rope. But to her surprise, they were already falling.

Lizzy held on tightly to Thorn as he grabbed onto the hook and removed it from the rock. They landed swiftly on their feet. "That was…surprisingly enjoyable!" Lizzy admitted.

They all looked down at the swampy lake full of toxic waste, dead fish, and garbage. "So…who's up for some scuba diving?" Thorn asked.

"No way! That water is dirtier than the sewage tunnel in Motherboard Fighters 3, Attack of the Gigabytes!"

Everyone looked at Scales like he had three heads. "What's that?" asked Geck.

"Motherboard Fighters is the ultimate Sci-Fi movie collection. The third one is where the character Flash discovers a glitch in the New York tunnel system. The evil scientist, Dr. Juan Circuit, is disguised as a sewer pipe worker. He locks Flash in the sewers and he has to live off of mud and toilet water for a week! Flash's friends, Sally and Marcus have to figure out how to hack into the main sewer canal gate to help Flash escape! It's my favorite out of all three movies!" Scales gushed.

"God bless you, Scales," Lizzy said quietly.

Camilia's hand was slipping. She looked down below to see some people talking, but they were too far below to see clearly. "There are four of them," she muttered to herself. Her hand slipped down the branch. Splinters were practically darting into her scales. Feeling faint, her hand finally opened.

She felt the weight of her body falling down, down. Her eyes closed and her body became loose and relaxed.

Thorn noticed the shadow of the moving figure on the ground; he looked up and squinted at the falling body. He opened out his arms and caught her, nearly slipping. Geck turned around and gasped, "Camilia?!" She ran over to Thorn. "How'd she get down here?"

Thorn looked downward at Camilia. "I'm not sure." He examined the splinters on her arm.

"Dude, is that Camilia?" Scales asked, very intrigued.

"I knew it! Camilia is an angel! That explains her perfect hair!" Lizzy gushed, touching Camilia's shoulder.

"Geck, call an ambulance. Once they get here, we hide and sneak onto the helicopter. Lizzy, you choke the pilot and throw him off the helicopter. Geck, you drive. Scales, collect all of Camilia's weapons, put them in a duffel bag, and throw them off the aircraft. Light the bag on fire first. That way, the bag should explode in midair. Geck, crash into the hospital and run over as many patients as you can. That way, none of the emergency rooms will be full. Lizzy, make sure you hide the bodies in their own separate bags before you drive back here and throw them into this river. Stab each bag multiple times to make sure they can't swim back up. I'll throw Camilia's unconscious body at a doctor to get his attention, then jump out the window and hide in a bush. Hopefully the bush will have enough needles. I might lose enough blood to die and stop moving. That way, I'll be harder to spot. Scales and Geck, get the blood off of the hospital floors to erase any evidence before the cops get there. Then, shoot every employee that isn't taking care of Camilia," Thorn explained his plan.

"Are you mad? That would never work! The hospital has security guards!" Geck yelled at him.

"I think it sounds like fun!" Scales defended him.

"Yes, and I think it sounds like jail!" Lizzy teased him.

"Okay, maybe I went too far with the helicopter," Thorn suggested.

"You went too far right after you told me to call an ambulance!" Geck said. "Fine, just call an ambulance," Thorn responded.

Geck's eyes grew wide once she looked at her phone screen. "No charge!" Geck shouted in anger. Her voice echoed throughout the canyon.

"You know," Thorn began.

"Don't you dare say a word, Thorn!" Geck yelled at him, "This is all your fault!"

"This is my fault because..."

"How did you expect us to get back up?"

"Guys," Scales called out to the others, "I dropped the hook and rope in the river by mistake."

"Cool, now we really are stuck here. These rocks are way too smooth and steep to climb! Everyone else's phone is out of charge," Geck sighed. "Thorn looked at his phone that was fully charged, and said nothing.

In the RV, Mishell was silently licking her lollipop. Tad was just looking out the window. "So...how are you feeling?" Tad asked Mishell.

"A lot better, actually! I think I can move again!"

"Oh, good, that deserves another lollipop!" Tad gushed, getting out her purse. But then they heard a strange moaning noise.

"What was that?" Mishell said, standing up.

"No, no, no!" Tad said, running to Mishell and pushing her down. "You have to rest, Ms. Mishell!"

They heard more moaning. It was getting louder. Mishell stood up and moved towards the small closet door in the back of the vehicle. She opened and nearly shrieked. Pyro was stuffed in there with blood all over his clothing. His skin was faded even more, and he looked terribly ill.

"Pyro?!" she cried. "Who did this to you?!" Pyro tried to breathe, but began to choke on the cold air from the open door. "Let me help you up," Mishell insisted. She reached out to touch his hand, but her finger was burnt immediately. "Ouch!" she yelped.

Mishell bent down and took a closer look at the blood. "Ignitodiles...blood..." she mumbled. "Your blood is partly lava, isn't it?" Mishell asked him. But, he was in too much pain to respond. "We're so sorry, Pyro. Tad told us you went to the gas station! Wait..."

She turned to Tad, who had the look of a child after she breaks her mother's vase. "Pyro, how'd you get in there?" Tad tried to play along.

"You...you traitor!" Mishell shouted at Tad. "You tricked us! Pyro didn't leave this van. You stuffed him in this closet and left him to rot! You evil...Amphibian!"

Tad was shocked. She touched herself on the chest. Tears ran down her cheeks.

Thorn looked in his satchel and got out his spare grappling hook. "You have a spare grappling hook?" Scales yelled.

REPTILES VS AMPHIBIANS

"Just remembered," Thorn replied, aiming at the top of the precipice.

He picked up the grappling hook and aimed it at the top of the cliff edge. Then, he pressed the trigger. The hook gripped onto the cork of the rock face. Geck took out her pager, to see if it was still functional. "Thorn, is your pager working?" she retorted. "I...don't know," he said, tightening the rope. "Could you see if it's connected to the Wi-Fi? Please?" she begged.

Thorn nodded and gave her the grappling hook, and then he took the pager. I don't see anything wrong with it," he said, about to push a button. "No, not that one!" Scales cried, but it was too late. Thorn had dropped onto the floor from the electrical shock.

"Okay, now we have two dead people to worry about!" Scales whined.

"Unconscious," Lizzy corrected him. Scales rolled his eyes and gave both girls a rope.

"Geck, you tie the rope around Thorn and yourself. Lizzy, tie the rope around Camilia and yourself."

The girls did what he said and picked up their satchels. "How come you're not carrying a body?" Lizzy asked.

"Do you really want to see me struggle with bodies five times heavier than me?"

That kept Lizzy quiet. They began to climb up the rope.

Eventually, they got up the cliff. Lizzy, Geck, and Scales got into the van, putting the bodies on the couch, but were taken by surprise.

"Pyro!" Scales cried, running to his dying brother with tears in his eyes. "How did this happen?" he asked Mishell quietly. Mishell said nothing, but sneaked a dirty look at Tad, who was still sitting on the floor crying.

Lizzy followed Scales to Pyro's decaying body. "Oh, what a tragedy!" she cried.

"Lizzy!" Scales yelled at her, "Could you shut up right now? We're trying to figure out something!" "Leave me alone! I feel just as bad as you do, but don't you think I should get a say in this?" "Just keep quiet! You don't know anything about this, do you?" Scales continued to scold her. "If you want my advice, I think you should stop crying and get an ambulance. I'd dial for them, but my phone's dead," Lizzy shrugged. "I'm pretty sure everyone else's phone is dead."

"I'm pretty sure nobody asked you, Lizzy. I don't even know why you're here. If you stayed home, there'd be no difference, so stop acting like you know what you're doing." Scales felt terrible for what he said, but he meant it.

CHAPTER 12

STANDING

"My phone's dead," Geck said with great sorrow.

Tad stood up. "There's a hospital about a mile from here."

"You've helped enough, Tad," Geck interrupted her, well aware of what she'd done.

"I still don't understand how Pyro got in here!" Scales complained, "And why is he all bloody and gross?"

"We can't ask questions now!" Geck told him, trying to be the new lead, "Who's driving?"

Scales sat in the driver's seat. "I'll drive."

"You're just a kid," Lizzy reminded him.

"I've disarmed an active nuke before. I've seen 33 episodes of *Chasers and Racers*. I'm an 8-year-old in high school. Not to toot my own horn, but I'm pretty sure I can drive a van."

Geck sat down on the passenger's seat, next to Scales. Mishell and Lizzy stayed by the bodies they had.

Tad sat by herself, still sobbing. Lizzy soon noticed this and sat beside her. "Tad, would you like to say something?"

"Yes. I've been a very naughty girl," Tad answered. "But I do have a reason for what I did!"

"You can tell me," Lizzy assured her.

"Okay. So, once you laid Pyro on the couch and left, I didn't know what to do. He told me not worry about him, but he asked me to bring him the empty cooler. I brought it to him, and he started to cough up blood."

Scales had already started driving, but he and Geck were listening intently.

"Pyro was coughing up blood for nearly three minutes! I felt so bad for him. I grabbed the bandages off the counter and started wrapping them around his leg. He pushed me away from him and told me to leave him alone. I was terrified. I had no idea why he wanted me to let him die.

"Pyro started to choke on a lump of his own blood. His phone was out of charge so I couldn't call 911. I noticed how much he was shivering, and I decided to get a blanket, but he resisted that too. After rolling around and moaning for a while, he just fell head first into the cooler. I heard a cracking noise and I was super scared. I called his name, but no response. He just sighed as his eyes closed.

"I simply decided to shut the cooler and let him rest. Then, I pulled the cooler in the closet, where it was warm. I didn't want you guys to worry, so I hid him at the back of the van, hoping he would wake up."

Lizzy blinked in disbelief. "Tad, Pyro was probably suffocating!"

Tad's cheeks glowed as red as a bloodshot cherry. The van came to a stop. Scales hopped off the driver's seat. "I told you I could drive!" he beamed.

"You crashed into a tree!" Mishell scolded him. "That's only because I couldn't reach the brakes and the steering wheel at the same time!" Scales protested.

Scales walked up to Tad. "I'm really sorry about your brother. My name is Tad. I'm Scat's niece. It's my fault that Pyro is like this," Tad explained.

"It's cool. I know you didn't mean to hurt him. Thanks for taking care of him. My name is Scales, by the way."

Scales turned to Geck and Lizzy. "Okay, we have to hide our identities. Take these." He threw two oversized black robes and politely handed one to Tad. "Put them on over your uniform just in case any Amphibians are around."

Geck and Lizzy put them on and waited outside with their hoods up. Scales put his hood on immediately. Tad just stared at hers, tears of remorse flowing off her cheeks. "What's wrong?" Scales asked. "Oh Scales, I can't come with you!" Tad cried.

"What? Why not? We might need your help!" Scales insisted.

"With what? All I've done was mess things up all day! I should've just stayed locked up in Uncle Scat's basement. He was right. I am a distraction."

"No you're not. You just think that because that's what your actions reflect. Pyro always tells me that for someone with such a big brain, I don't think at all. Maybe we both need to start thinking before we act. What do you say?"

Scales waited for an answer. But Tad just gave him the cloth and covered her face. Scales ran to the door.

"That's fine. You could believe in what your uncle tells you. It's not like I can stop you," Scales said and then hopped out of the vehicle.

"You're kind of like your brother," Lizzy told him, putting her hood over her head. "So?" Scales mumbled as he started dragging the cooler into the hospital.

Geck picked up the duffel bag with Camilia's body in it and followed. Lizzy picked up the duffel bag with Thorn's body and came right behind them.

In the hospital, two nurses were at the front desk. "How can we help you…?" One said, noticing the three hooded people.

Scales pointed down at the two bags and the cooler. Then, he, Lizzy, and Geck left out the door. They waited a few minutes for Thorn, Camilia, and Pyro to be taken to the emergency room.

"I'm going to check on the others," Mishell said, getting out of the van. Tad looked out the window, and then took out a strange, pager-like object. "Come in head guard!" she whispered into the speaker. "Present," a lady told her through the device. "What is your progress, agent?"

"I have endangered three out of four of them so far. The fourth one recently had a discussion with Scat." Tad responded.

"Very well, you have one hour to destroy the redhead."

"I shall try, ma'am. By the way, what time is it?"

"7:50 p.m. Good luck, agent," The voice said. She hung up.

Tad took a deep breath, and then exhaled. "I have one hour to get rid of Geck," Tad reassured herself, "I can do this."

Mishell, who was secretly eavesdropping next to the window, was overwhelmed with shock. "She meant to hurt them?" Mishell muttered to herself, "But how?"

After 30 minutes, Geck, Lizzy, and Scales climbed the back stairs and sneaked through the hospital window. There, they saw Thorn lying on the hospital bed, eyes closed, and covered with a blanket.

"Thorn, you're not dead!" Lizzy beamed reaching out to touch Thorn, but his eyes popped open and he clutched onto her wrist. Lizzy squealed and struggled to break free from his intense grip.

"Thorn, you're okay?" Geck's eyes grew wide. She hugged him tightly.

"I literally just bashed my head against a 5 ton boulder and scraped my face against razor sharp pebbles covered with sand and red ants. Yes, Geck, I'm okay," Thorn said sarcastically.

"Good! I have no idea what happened back there. Scales must've done something to our pagers. Wait, if you were just in a concussion, how would you remember that?"

"Geck," Thorn told her, lifting up the bangs from his forehead. The bandage tied around his head was now visible. "I might know why all of this happened." He sat up, "Camilia falling off the cliff, Pyro being stabbed, and me, passing out. Someone must've sabotaged us."

"Yeah, but how could someone sabotage us without knowing

what we're doing?" Lizzy asked, still trying to break free from Thorn's grip.

Thorn finally let her go. "My apologies, I hate being touched." He got out a dusty old book from behind the hospital bed.

"Has anything strange happened today?" he asked Geck.

"Well, Pyro was stabbed, Mishell was kidnapped, I was sent a threatening text message, Camilia mysteriously fell out of the sky, and we found Pyro in a cooler…"

"Wait, you said you received a threatening text message?"

"Yeah, around 6:20 p.m.," Geck said.

"What was this text message?"

"I remember it was from this girl named Charlotte from our school."

"Did the text message have anything to do with revealing a secret?"

"Yes, it did! How'd you know?"

"A great percentage of threatening messages, verbal or manuscript, that are sent to secret agents are either death threats or threats to reveal one's 'secret.'"

Scales shrugged and murmured, "What does that have to do with anything?"

Thorn opened the book. "Luck…" he began to read, "something that happens by chance rather than rational consequences."

"I still don't get it," Scales said.

"Was it rational for me, Pyro, and Camilia to all be put in the hospital at the exact same day and time, but for different reasons?"

"I suppose not," Lizzy replied.

"So, this may be described as bad luck, or an event that occurred just by chance."

He turned the page. "Coincidence; the state of happening at the same time or being identical or the fact of happening without planning. A coincidence might be that three people who all know each other end up in the same hospital for different reasons."

"Geck, you pushed me and I fell, but it wasn't specifically your fault. You were still under the control of Scat, weren't you?" Geck really didn't know, but she didn't want to seem clueless in front of her friends, and she nodded slightly.

"As for Camilia, I am aware of her fear of being kidnapped. When the ninjas left Scales stranded, they must've tried to kidnap her. Camilia most likely had a panic attack, causing her to harm the driver in some way. Because of the driver not paying attention on a bumpy passage way, the vehicle must've been in a horrific accident, causing the van to tip over and Camilia to fall out, roll off a cliff, and grab onto a branch. The ninjas must've retreated to their base. After a while, we showed up about half a mile from where Scales was left and where the damaged van was abandoned," Thorn reminded. "We later slid down the rope and once we got to the bottom of the cliff, Camilia let go of the branch. She fell and I caught her," Thorn told them.

"Oh, that makes sense!" Scales grinned. "Yes, and Pyro was stabbed when Gallant and two other ninjas fought him in order to take Mishell away. Pyro eventually became exhausted from the blood loss and collapsed. But soon after he woke up, he tried limping to where Mishell was, but ran into us," Geck recalled.

"I think I understand now," Lizzy smiled, "Whoever has been sabotaging us must've predicted the possibility of any of that happening!"

Thorn sensed a sharp ache in his head. He ducked down quickly. "Thorn, are you okay?" Geck asked him. "Migraine..." he mumbled. "I'm fine. You must go and find Pyro and Camilia. Make sure they're alright."

Scales, Geck, and Lizzy nodded simultaneously. They donned their hoods and went to the front desk.

One man wearing a lab coat turned around. "How may I assist

you today?"

"Three visitor's passes, please," Geck requested.

"Ma'am, no children allowed," he said looking at Scales suspiciously.

Scales tried to lower his voice. "Um...I'm not a kid, I'm a midget!"

The man raised an eyebrow. "Very well, who would you like to visit?"

"Do you have a Camilia Veildson?" Lizzy asked.

The doctor scowled at her. "Oh...a Reptile," he murmured, handing them their passes.

"That was strange! Why was that guy upset about Camilia being a Reptile?" Geck wondered out loud.

Scales did not respond. Lizzy began to whistle. "Guys, why aren't you answering?" Geck mumbled.

"You don't know, do you?" Lizzy asked dourly.

"What don't I know?" Geck asked.

"Nothing," Scales told her. They entered Room 101.

"Camilia!" Geck cried, running to the side of the bed. Camilia was lying down, dressed in a hospital gown. Her left leg was tied in a cast. She was just staring at the wall, lonely-looking, and tired. But then she noticed her best friend at the side of the bed, and her face lightened up. "Geck! How'd you get here?"

"We came to visit you!"

"What happened to my leg?"

"You fell off a cliff and survived."

"What are Scales and Lizzy doing here?"

"They came with me."

Scales followed Geck to the end of the hospital bed. "I think somebody owes me a debt of gratitude! You know, for almost risking my life for that person?" He reminded Camilia.

Camilia sat up. "Okay, come here, sweetie." Scales went next to her, and she kissed him on the cheek. Scales blushed immediately. "I would've taken a 'thanks' but I guess that's cool too."

"We just wanted to make sure you're not hurt badly," Lizzy explained.

"My leg still hurts when I move it, but I think I'll be okay," Camilia said.

"Good. Let's go check on Pyro now," Scales insisted.

"I think Pyro's in the room right next to this one," Camilia told them. Geck hugged Camilia and led the others out of the room.

They entered room 102. There, Pyro was talking with a nurse. "I don't care if I should eat more! I need to know when I can walk again!" Pyro argued with his caretaker.

"Listen dear; I keep saying that you'll need to rest for a couple of days!" The nurse protested and left the room.

Pyro tried getting up. "Ow!" he yelped.

Lizzy, Geck, and Scales confronted him. "Pyro, are you okay? If you're going be stuck here forever, can I have your room?!" Scales yelled.

"No I'm not okay," Pyro protested stubbornly, folding his arms, "I have to sit here for the next couple of weeks. This is so unfair! Not only do I have to die here, but this room has no TV!"

"On a related note, there are starving children in Africa. Stop whining and get over it, you big baby!" Geck scolded him.

"Scales, what happened to you and Camilia?" Pyro asked Scales.

"I was dropped out of a van in the woods and Camilia fell off a cliff. She's okay, though."

They heard the nurse's footsteps. "We have to leave," Lizzy said.

"See you in a few weeks, bro," Scales smiled. Pyro smiled back. No matter how bad the situation was, he couldn't be mad at someone who really cared.

Once the nurses came back in, Pyro gave her a scowl. "Look, I'm sorry I can't help you, but you can help yourself to a lollipop." The nurse smirked, handing him a jar of candy. "Take as many as you want!"

Pyro was getting fed up with the nurse mocking him. "I do not want anything to eat! I'm not hungry!"

"Child, you weigh 50 lbs.! You need food!"

"No, I don't! Can you please just tell me if I can walk again?"

"Your wrist is the width of a pencil!" the nurse told him.

Pyro's eyes lit a bloodshot red color. When the nurse noticed this, she knew what she was dealing with. It was a misfit. It was an Ignitodile.

Geck, Lizzy, and Scales got back inside the van. Tad was sitting quietly, playing with her dolls. She kept staring at Geck. "Hi, Tad. Are you...having fun, there?" Geck said to her as friendly as she could.

Tad pulled out a blade knife from her pocket. "Look behind you!" Lizzy called out. Geck turned around, and Tad threw the blade. Luckily, Geck sensed the knife about to touch her neck, and ducked. The blade caused a crack in the window.

"Tad...you threw that?" Lizzy asked.

Mishell ran into the van. "Yes, she did! I saw her! She was on a walkie-talkie with some woman! She's planning to kill you, Geck!"

Tad said nothing, but just stared at the floor. "Tad, how could you?" Scales looked at her with pain in his eyes. He and Lizzy shielded Geck. Geck was also speechless. She just kept gazing at Tad with disgust.

Mishell crossed her arms and glared at Tad. "So, you not only caused the death of hundreds, but also locked Pyro in a closet, and tried to assassinate Geck? What type of innocent little girl are you?"

Tad just sighed and put her dolls down. Scales was starting to get annoyed with her. "So, you've been with the Amphibians the entire time? You were just pretending to be some harmless kid? You've been working alongside your uncle this whole time, haven't you? Or is he even your uncle?"

Tad just looked up at him and said quietly, "You're making me feel bad."

"Good. Now you know how it feels," Scales said, returning to the driver's seat.

Geck finally spoke, "For a minute, you reminded me of myself, someone who wants to help out and someone who no one will listen to, but I see clearly that we are nothing alike."

"Don't talk to me!" Tad shrieked.

Lizzy took Tad's purse with all of her weapons in it, and threw it out the window. Tad was then tied up with an old rope. "You're very lucky the Reptilian policy does not permit abandonment or abduction," Mishell told her, "otherwise, we could've left you where the ninjas left Scales!"

Everyone sat down. "Where are you taking me?" Tad asked with fear in her eyes.

"Back to the temple, the Amphibian base is where you belong," Scales replied and drove off.

They arrived in front of the large golden building. Tad was untied and escorted by Scales off of the van. "You know, we could've been friends," Scales sighed as they approached the door.

CHAPTER 13

SURVIVING

Scales was hurting about it, but he was too upset to express how he felt. But as for Tad, her tears never stopped flowing.

Neither of the two had a friend their own age. But coincidentally, they were 8-year-olds doing adult work. Tad was heartbroken by that statement. She was starting to like Scales. "I'm an Amphibian. You're a Reptile. We could never be friends," she replied, opening the door.

Scales turned and walked off before Tad could even shut the door. He hopped onto the van. "I'll drop you off, Geck. Then we'll have to go back to the South Campus. This mission is ending a little bit early."

Scales stepped on the gas pedal. The car zoomed off.

Three weeks later, Geck woke up in her dorm room. She looked across the room to see that Camilia's bed was empty, but then she thought to herself, "Oh yeah, it's Saturday! Thorn, Camilia, and Pyro should be out of the hospital by now!"

She sprung from the bed and rushed into the girls' freshmen and sophomores' room, which was right across the hall from the girls' juniors and seniors' room.

Geck rushed to the sink and started brushing her teeth rapidly, getting toothpaste everywhere. Other girls were starting to stare at her like she was crazy. Geck finished gargling the water and spat it out on the girl right next to her. "Sorry!" She called out, grabbing her clothes and running towards the shower and spa area.

Geck sprinted into one of the showers, still wearing her pajamas, and not realizing that it was occupied by someone else. It was Diane, who was luckily wearing her towel.

"My bad!" Geck said, soaking wet, and turning to leave.

But Diane grabbed her arm. "Not so fast, Reptile, you're not aware of what I've done, are you?"

Geck rolled her eyes and replied, "Well, you've squeezed most of my blood out through my arm."

"Oh, Geck, you and your friends are not as innocent as you think you are. We all know your dirty little secret."

"Look, I don't want trouble. I just came to shower!"

"You ignored the text message that Charlotte sent you!" Diane reminded her.

"I was doing something important!" Geck insisted.

Diane's wicked glare turned into a delighted smile faster than a lightning bolt next to a metal pole. "Really? And what might that be?"

Geck gulped, "I was at a dentist appointment...?"

"You have to have teeth to go to the dentist!"

"Let go of me!" Geck yelled as she socked Diane in the stomach with her knee.

"Ow! You can't hide from a secret, Geck!" Diane shouted. Geck ran away from the curtain in shame. All of the other girls were putting on their towels and shower caps, but at the same time sneaking mean looks at Geck.

Geck went to the shower all the way in a dark corner that no one used. It was perfectly clean and working, but nobody ever seemed to notice it. Geck removed her slippers. She sat down on a lonely bench, removing her socks, then, her sweater. As she undressed, she thought of what the 'dirty little secret' that Diane was talking about could be.

"Maybe it's about how I sometimes bite my toenails," Geck said to herself, "Or maybe it's about how I snore really loudly when I sleep."

Geck undid her hair. She couldn't think of any more secrets... except for one. One dreadful secret that nobody in the whole entire school could know besides her, Camilia, Thorn, and Pyro. The secret of how they all worked for the agency of the Reptiles. There could be no possible way for Diane to just find out.

Geck wrapped her towel around her shoulders to keep warm. She put her hair back up into pigtails as fast as she could and hurried out the door.

Geck quickly scampered into the elevator at the end of the hall. As soon as the door closed, she punched the wall. Once the wallpaper tore, a dusty, old button with the letter "B" was there. She pressed it. The elevator opened, and she was in the dark, rusty, lair. It was pretty cold, so she rested the towel on her shoulders and continued walking.

Geck approached the table and searched through a bunch of papers. After five minutes of checking, she gasped. The papers that Thorn got from Mr. Beasley's room were gone! "He left it under these papers!" Geck said out loud.

"I guess Thorn's not very good at hiding things," a voice said. Geck turned around to see Diane in a bathrobe, smiling sinisterly in the dramatic lighting.

"Diane, you didn't take the files, did you?" Geck asked.

"As much as I love lying, I actually stumbled upon a rusty old elevator at the end of the hall that said, 'out of order' three weeks ago. The same week when you ignored Charlotte's text! She was bluffing. She knew nothing about your secret," Diane clarified. "But I found the elevator while sneaking into your dorm and finding a letter. It read 'elevator passage' in bright red. I followed the map to the elevator. Then, I found your little hideout, and then the papers!"

"Diane, you didn't tell anyone, did you?!" Geck panicked.

"Relax! I didn't tell anyone directly. I just read it...on the P.A.!"

Geck thought she was magically going to transform into a volcano and erupt. "Everyone in school knows about the agency?" Geck asked.

"Yes! By the way, you missed the dance. I won! It was great... for me."

Geck couldn't take it anymore. "Diane, what did we ever do to you? I know you hate me and everything, but why are you picking on my friends now? What about Pyro? Do you still like him?"

Diane giggled. "You're an idiot even when you're upset! Of course I still like Pyro. That's why once the whole school turns against you and the other Reptiles, I'll be the one to support and care for Pyro, while he'll be angry at you for ignoring Charlotte's text!"

"Diane, Pyro despises you. How could he ever like you? He'll hate you for being the one to ruin our lives and revealing our secret!"

"Even if Pyro doesn't like me, at least I got voted Queen of the Freshman Dance!"

"You got what you wanted, Diane. Why are you torturing us now?"

Diane opened the elevator button. "Just for fun!" she gushed. The elevator door shut. The loud clanging noise the doors made matched the exact same way Geck felt in her heart; hard and outmoded.

Tad lay down on the hard, freezing ground of the Temple basement. Every time she sniffed, a teardrop fell onto the concrete surface. All she could do was think of how much she'd hurt her friends. She thought about how Scales "could've been" one of those friends. Scales was the only other child she'd ever seen let alone talked to in years.

Then, the door creaked open. A soldier marched down the stairs to talk to her. "Tad, the head guard demands to speak with you!" Tad stood immediately. She was in trouble.

Tad entered a room with dim lighting and shut windows. A young lady was sitting in a chair and filing her nails. "You failed..." she mumbled.

"I know, but Geckeliette! Her reflexes are above average!" Tad whined. "I'm just a child!"

The lady's chair spun around. It was Iguan.

"I'm letting you off the hook, for now. Just remember that I'm watching you. You need to stay away from the Reptiles. I'm aiming the missiles at them. We are going to turn every being in Phenise against them."

"I don't understand! I thought you wanted to be good!" Tad told her.

"I did..." Iguan replied, standing up, "but then I thought...what good is it being good if you're not doing any good? The Reptiles take care of every single mishap on Creatoigin, so it's not like I can do much." Iguan put her nail filer down.

"Then I looked on the bright side. My father is an idiot. I figured I could use that against him. I decided to deprive him of the one thing that made sense...his goals!" she chuckled.

"Inform my father that my bags are packed," Iguan said, pointing to another Amphibian.

He nodded and left. "So, you're leaving?"

"You two-face! Don't ask me about leaving. Of course I'm leaving. My dad was right. I am getting older. I need to grow up. All I need to do is get my own house, drop out of high school, and maybe change the name he gave me." Iguan clarified, "Anyway, I figured that my father's goals are to turn everyone against the Reptiles, get everybody on his side, and eventually destroy the Reptiles. That way, he can steal anything he wants without anyone stopping him. I've done some thinking, and I've decided...I want that too. And I'm not going to let my dad get in the way of that. Therefore, I must turn everyone against the Reptiles before him. His way obviously isn't working, so I've decided to do it my way!"

"Iguan, Uncle Scat loves you!" Tad tried to convince her.

Iguan didn't react directly. She just continued to stare judgingly. "Go back downstairs. You're useless," she commanded.

Tad left, slamming the door.

Geck pressed the elevator button. The door opened and she walked into the elevator. She dialed Mishell's number on her cell. "Hello?" Mishell asked. She sounded as if she had just woken up.

"Mishell, today's the day. Tell Scales to pick me up at 10:00 a.m."

"Don't stay out too long. You know who's after you."

"Tad is a little girl."

"So are you! She's working for Scat. You never know what that guy has under his sleeve, probably a pistol."

"I'll be fine, Mishell," Geck laughed, hanging up.

An hour later, Geck was outside in her favorite panda bear hoodie and jeans, waiting for the van. "It's freezing out here…" Geck murmured. Two kids in her class walked by, starring at her in awe. One had braces and was wearing suspenders. The other wore glasses and a bowtie.

"Hi, Ben! Hi, Jack!" Geck smiled at them. Ben whispered something in Jack's ear.

"Ben, that's not very courteous!" Jack giggled.

"What is it?" Geck stopped smiling.

"Oh…nothing," Ben sighed. They continued walking, but Geck kept following them.

"No, seriously! Tell me! Everybody I see has been giving me strange looks lately. I don't know why!"

"How desperate are you to find out?" Jack snorted.

"I…I'll hug you guys!" Geck said, trying to convince him.

Jack looked at Ben. "Well, there's been a rumor going around in school."

"Yeah," Ben added, adjusting his suspenders, "It's about you…

and Thorn, Camilia, and Pyro. People are saying that you guys are secret agents or something."

"Secret agents?" Geck mumbled.

"But we know it's not true, right?" Jack questioned her, taking off his glasses and wiping them against his shirt.

"Did...Diane spread that rumor by any chance?" Geck asked them.

"Yeah," Ben elucidated, "she was reading something about a secret organization called the 'Reptiles'. She also mentioned how ironic it was that you and your friends are all half reptiles. Like how you have green skin and a large gecko tail sticking out from your sweater."

Geck blushed. She didn't like it when people mentioned her tail. Jack noticed her embarrassment. "But, it's a very pretty sweater! I like it!"

"Thanks..." Geck muffled her voice. Then she remembered how her secret was in danger. "Um...I have to go..." Geck said.

She was about to turn to leave, but she hugged the two of them tightly first. "I might be gone for a while..." Geck told them. "I know the whole school probably knows about this, I need you guys not to make it worse. Don't tell anyone else, but...we *are* spies." Geck finally broke the hug and sprinted off.

Jack and Ben were dumbfounded. "Did she just hug me?" Jack asked Ben.

"Forget that! She said she was a spy!" Ben said nudging him in the stomach. They watched her darting off into the distance.

"She's cute when she's running," Jack gushed. Ben just rolled his eyes.

"We have to keep this secret from the whole school. Geck's counting on us, so don't let your big mouth get in the way or she'll never talk to us again!"

Jack and Ben nodded, and went back inside the school.

Geck ran to the RV parked on the curb. She opened the door and ran in. She slammed the door shut and collapsed on the floor, out of breath. "What's up with you?" Scales asked.

"They know," Geck replied sharply. Then she made a triangle with her fingers.

Scales gasped and shivered a little bit. "Oh, okay..." he mumbled sadly, starting the engine. "We'll just have to get to the hospital ASAP, now won't we?" He put the engine on drive. The motor roared. The car started moving right away.

At the hospital, Geck hopped out of the car and hugged Camilia as snugly as she could. Camilia immediately hugged her back. She had two metal crutches. "I missed you so much!" Camilia gushed.

"Same!" Geck uttered. "What's up with the crutches?"

"These aren't just any crutches. These are the new techno crutches that everyone is talking about! If I press this button," Camilia said, pointing to a green button on one of the crutches, "the sticks fold up into cubes that can fit in your pocket! The blue button turns the crutches into rocket boots!"

But then Geck broke the hug and said, "They know," and made a triangle with her fingers.

Camilia's eyes widened. Her grin disappeared. "I understand. Pyro and Thorn are in the lobby," Camilia sighed. "I didn't think it would be today..." They both entered the building.

There, Thorn sat on a couch, legs crossed and meditating. The bandage still remained tied around his forehead.

Pyro was on the opposite end of the couch, reading his comics. Geck and Camilia looked at each other, and at the boys. "Hey, Geck!" Pyro smiled at her. Thorn just waved quietly.

"The doctors gave me these cool fingerless gloves to help me conceal my flame spawning abilities. They should block out most of the air from my palms, so that way I can't make fire easily!" Pyro exclaimed, showing them his hands.

REPTILES VS AMPHIBIANS

"Guys, we have some bad news," Camilia tried to tell them gently.

"I don't have to stay for three more weeks, do I?"

"No, pay attention!" Geck scolded him.

"What happened?" Thorn questioned them, opening his eyes.

Camilia and Geck both said in unison, "They know." Both of them made a triangle with their fingers.

Thorn sat up. "It's today?"

"I guess so," Camilia replied.

Pyro's eyes became crossed. "What does that mean again?"

Geck sighed hopelessly, "It means that we have to blow up the school, moron."

"I guess I forgot," Pyro said, "but it hasn't happened for so long!"

"If our communications systems are still hacked, we might have to blow up more than the school. Maybe the entire country of Phenise," Thorn explained to him.

Pyro stopped smiling. "So if we destroyed Phenise, where would we live?" he asked, "And why would we blow up the school, let alone the country? We have so many friends!"

Camilia touched his shoulder. "Let's not worry about that now."

Thorn stood up. "Let's head to the van."

Camilia, Thorn, and Geck left. Pyro picked up his crutches and followed behind them.

In the van, Scales was lying down on the couch, thinking. "Are you okay, buddy?" Pyro asked, sitting next to him.

"I'm fine, I guess. I just didn't think all of this would happen so soon," Scales told him.

Pyro hugged his brother. "And we're going to make sure you stay okay."

Scales nodded and smiled. "You know, you're kind like me...in a way, I guess," Pyro smiled back. "Yeah, I get that a lot," Scales said.

Thorn made a circle with his fingers. Pyro, Camilia, and Geck approached him right away. "This is a very solemn time of our lives. We have all lived good lives, but they will never be the same. You all must remember that we were put in the same team to work with each other, not against each other."

"I remember when we first became a team," Camilia said, trying to bring back happy memories, "We were all so young. We didn't know what the future held for us. I remember how Thorn taught me how to hold a katana."

"Oh yeah!" Pyro added, "I was afraid of everything! I didn't want to do any work, until Camilia kept yelling at me. Now I'm an awesome fighter...and deaf in one ear."

"Yeah," Geck joined in, "I never even thought we could be a team! I didn't know we could go a day being a team, let alone five years! Pyro encouraged me to stay at the camp, even though I missed my home so much!"

"I remember how Geck was the one that helped me sneak into Sensei Sudoku's bedroom and read his diary. I learned all of my moves from reading it. After that, I started to enjoy reading," Thorn replied.

Scales, who was still lying down, fell asleep. He was dreaming about a world where he and his team members wouldn't be in danger every day.

"We've come a long way," Thorn told them, "Breaking the bond that we have now could cause this whole island to fall apart. No matter what everyone says, we must focus on our own opinions. We will adjust as a team. We will accept who we are as a team. Even if the world is against us, we will stay together and face them...as a team."

The van drove off.

ABOUT THE AUTHOR: MINI BIOGRAPHY

Name: Chelcie C. Oparanozie

Born: January 11th, 2003

Birth Place: Elizabeth, New Jersey

First Book: Reptiles vs. Amphibians (2015)

Genre: Sci-fi, action/adventure, comedy, romance/drama

Favorite Color: Turquoise

Favorite Food: Cheese cake (preferably chocolate)

Inspiration: Chelcie got the inspiration from her grandma, who also writes religious books. Chelcie enjoys writing fiction because it allows her imagination to let loose and roam free. Chelcie was also inspired by the cartoons she watched as a small child. She loved to write little fan-fictions and parodies when she was around six years old. Chelcie would turn them into small booklets. She liked to keep them to herself and read them all the time. One day, her sister, Daisy took one of her booklets to school by mistake. The teacher ended up reading it to her and her preschool class. They all loved it so much; the teacher asked if she could keep it for the class. Chelcie said yes, of course. It made her feel good that sharing her imagination made others happy. Then she thought to herself, *If people like me writing about other characters, what if I made my own original characters and wrote about them?*

From then on, Chelcie began creating, drawing, and writing about her own original characters. Pretty soon, her dad told her that she needed to start writing on the computer like a real author.

At first Chelcie said no. The last time she wrote on a computer, her parents couldn't get the marker off! But, eventually, she ended up writing her first book...and you're reading it!

CPSIA information can be obtained
at www.ICGtesting.com
Printed in the USA
FFOW02n1102160216
21538FF

9 780997 033465